Darker Waters
MERMAIDENS
2

Enrapturing Tales is an imprint of:

Knight Writing Press
PMB # 162
13009 S. Parker Rd.
Parker CO 80134
knightwritingpress.com
KnightWritingPress@gmail.com

Cover Art and Cover Design © 2025 Ruth Nickle

Other Interior Art © 2022, 2025 Knight Writing Press

Additional Copyright Information can be found on page 217

Interior Book Design and eBook Design by Knight Writing Press

Editor Jessica Guernsey
Executive Editor Sam Knight

First Publication January 2025

Paperback ISBN-13: 978-1-62869-071-2
eBook ISBN-13: 978-1-62869-072-9

Table of Contents

A Note from the Editor

*M*y mom always hated *The Little Mermaid*. And now that I'm older, I get it. You don't love him. You just met him! And yes, at 16, you are still a child! In college, I did my final project for a mythology class on how Disney got Hans Christian Anderson's tale all wrong. Mermaids are still fascinating to me. And not just the ones with flowing locks and glimmering tails.

Sirens lure men to their deaths. Greek Naiads are water nymphs who play in streams and rivers. Melusine are the two-tailed mermaids made popular by a Seattle coffee brand. Lamia will sometimes have a serpent tail along with their penchant for eating children. The German tale of Lorelei was a woman scorned who drowned herself, thus becoming the siren of the Rhine River.

Not all mermaids are beautiful. The Japanese Ningyo was notoriously ugly, a large fish with a human face. Myths say its flesh grants immortality. The Irish Merrow has beautiful females, true, but their males are quite hideous. Never cross a Merrow as their tempers cause storms. Scylla, the legendary monster from *The Odyssey*, was once a beautiful nymph, but according to mythology, was changed into a multi-headed monster with a tail.

And what else do most mermaid myths and stories have in common? Death and destruction. Ran, a Scandinavian sea goddess, causes awful shipwrecks. Slavic Rusalka are more demon than human, the souls of drowned maidens that bewitch those that come too close. The African Mami Wata is said to be as beautiful as she is dangerous and must be appeased with offerings to assure safe passage.

I find it interesting that cultures around the world have stories of merfolk. Beautiful. Beguiling. Baleful. Is it any wonder that our fascination with these otherworldly creatures inspires stories? Step a toe in the water and listen to the sirens sing. Swim in these darker waters.

- Jessica Guernsey
January 2025

Monster of the Deep

by

Sara K. Anderson

Monster of the Deep

S alt water caressed Ashera's feet.
Her cursed, ugly feet.
"Molly!"
The name sent a visceral reaction through her body, and a sudden urge to upend her morning meal into the sea foam crawled up her throat.

"Molly, darling?" Clay called for her again, his footsteps coming from the direction of the manor—that horrible dry place that leeched the moisture from her flesh.

Ashera did not speak.

Not to him.

Never to him.

Sand whispered behind her as he approached. His hands, large and firm, gripped her shoulders. They could crush her bones if they tightened further.

"Did you not hear me, love?"

Her silence was the only weapon she claimed for herself.

Clay turned her toward him, tearing her away from the sea.

It wasn't the first time.

"Molly?"

Ashera refused to meet his gaze. He laughed, the sound of it a warning. In her mind, his open maw was akin to the grin of a shark. A thick golden chain hung from his neck, a large sea-green stone dangling from it. She glared at the gem.

"The carriage is here." Clay ran a rough finger down her cheek. His scent was thick between them, that smokey substance he packed into his pipe clinging to every fiber of his high collared waistcoat.

"Once you are free of the pull, you will see the good I've done," he said. "You will see that I am right. There is so much more to the world, Molly. It'll be an adventure."

Ashera closed her eyes, listening as waves built and crashed. Beneath them, voices called to her. Their song matched the yearning in her chest. It stoked a fire within her that burned hotter than any in the manor's cursed hearths.

An adventure? She laughed bitterly to herself. *No, not an adventure, Clay Burton.*

A death sentence.

Ashera stood at the fringes of the ballroom, the low buzz of electric lights an underlying hum. People laughed and spoke with words so loud her eardrums might burst. Her eyes watered, the bright artificial light fogging the edges of her vision. She swiped a gloved hand over them. The fan hanging from her wrist swung, useless and tedious as a tangle of seaweed.

The dress she wore made every breath strenuous. Even though she'd smacked the maid who had tightened the stays, the woman had ignored her and tightened them further. Ashera picked at her skirts. The deep green silk gleamed, almost undulating beneath the sparkle of the chandeliers. It reminded her of home, and therefore, was the garment's only redemptive feature.

"How strange she is."

"I've never seen skin so pale."

"Or eyes so large."

"Do you see that? The sheen of her hair is green. How unsightly."

"Yes, and her dress! The neckline is so high she would be welcome in a nunnery."

Even if Ashera did not have sensitive ears, she would have heard them. They spoke behind unfurled fans, as if doing so made up for the poison lacing their words. They wanted her to hear them.

So she met their eyes and grinned a dark, feral grin. Like an eel—wide and carnivorous. They squealed, then fluttered their fans to cool flushed faces before scuttling away like a cast of crabs.

Ashera traced an absent finger along the high collar of her dress, itching to undo the pearl buttons. She closed her eyes, listening past the din of the ballroom.

Nothing. Only an aching, awful silence that chilled her bones. They were so far from the ocean now, staying in the heart of Lierian, miles and miles from her home. The city was made of smoke, oil, and ash. It clung to her skin and filled her lungs. Disgusting, dirty, foul—

"Molly, must you be so taciturn?"

I must, she thought, looking over Clay's charcoal gray tailcoat and frilly cravat spilling from his neck like lionfish fins. Ashera could not see the dark gem, but she knew he wore it tucked away somewhere.

She could feel it.

She rubbed a hand over her chest.

The orchestra began to play, and people paired off to dance.

"Dance with me." Clay claimed her hand, pulling her close. "We both know how much you love music."

She hissed, and he chuckled. "Enchanting as the day we met, my love."

Ashera almost lunged for him, almost sunk her teeth—but, no. She needed answers first.

A prickling crawled up her spine. Someone was watching her.

Someone other than the hordes of judging stares from lords and ladies.

Clay turned her about, colorful gowns bleeding into each other. A pair of dark eyes caught her gaze; a young man on the fringes of the ballroom, back straight. Ashera recognized him as Clay's manservant, standing to attention amongst others of his kind.

She remembered his name because she'd almost laughed when she'd heard it. Finn. The name of fish appendages.

Finn did not glare at her as the ladies did, or gaze upon her with open desire like Clay and many other men. His eyes held a determination that made her wary.

"Look at *me*, Molly darling." Although Clay's words were sweet, his voice was not. Kin to the growl of one of his hunting dogs. She hated those beasts; sniffing her out every time she tried to hide away from Clay's hungry gaze.

"So much malice in their depths," he said, grinning. "You *will* come around, my love. And you will speak to me with that haunting voice of yours. I'll coax it from you yet."

Wax dripped onto Ashera's finger. She bit back a yelp, almost dropping the candle. The candle had already been short, and the wick had completely burnt down during her search, wax pooling in the little brass plate until it spilled over. She set it down on a nearby table, its meager light casting flickering shadows over the books lining the walls.

So many of the cursed things. She wanted to tear them from the shelves and rip them all to shreds. Perhaps she would, after she found what she was looking for.

Moonlight peeked through, the heavy curtains not quite drawn all the way over. The library had many shelves and curved alcoves. Between the shelves were tall arched windows.

The candle went out with a soft sizzle, a thin strand of smoke barely visible in the darkness. She preferred the dark, even if her eyes had changed into useless night-blind orbs.

The sound of the large library doors being carefully opened and guided shut whispered in the silence, followed by a soft *scuff, scuff* of booted feet.

Ashera lifted the brass candle holder and backed up till her back pressed against the nearest bookshelf. She'd bludgeon whoever came into view.

The shuffling feet paused. Shadows bloomed. A lantern had been lit, the light swaying as they approached once more. She took a deep breath through her nose, but Clay's pungent, smokey scent was absent. One of the servants then? A hand came into view, holding the lantern high. Ashera slammed the brass holder into their wrist. The stranger cried out; the lantern crashing to the marble tiles. The light went out in an instant, drowning them in darkness as Ashera grabbed the intruder and slammed them into the wall.

Ashera clamped a hand over their mouth and spoke her first words since leaving her home.

"I will kill you if you breathe a word to him that I was here." The words rolled awkwardly off her tongue, but she managed. Everything about her body was different now, even her vocal cords; not to mention the weeks of silence lent her words a husky tone from disuse.

The stranger was still as stone, and after a moment, Ashera's eyes adjusted to the darkness, soft moonlight spilling through cracks in the curtains.

Finn.

"Swear it." Ashera bared her teeth as she lifted her hand away. "Swear it, or I'll rip your tongue out."

Finn grabbed her wrists.

She hissed and squirmed, but he only tightened his grip. "Hush, I'm not here to harm you. I swear I will not tell Master Burton."

Ashera stiffened. "Then why are you here? Why not tell your master you found me snooping?"

He released her wrists and leaned close, his dark hair wild from their scuffle. "What you seek is not here."

"You know what I seek?" Ashera asked.

Finn pressed his lips together, as if debating whether to tell her. His jaw flexed, and he nodded. "I do."

"Do you know where it is?"

"Yes." His hesitation was gone, replaced by that steely determination she'd seen in the ballroom.

"Will you tell me?" she asked.

"Better. I'll retrieve it for you."

She clenched a hand over her chest, gripping her nightgown. "Why? Why help me?"

Finn leaned in even more, their faces so close she could smell tea leaves and honey whispering from his lips. "Wild things should not be caged. And you *are* a wild thing. Your presence has turned the young master mad, and he will not come to his senses until you are gone. So I'll say it again. What you seek is not here, and if you had half a mind, you would know he would not leave something like that where anyone could find it."

He was so close—his breath warm on her skin. There was a darkness to him that pulled at her like the depths of the sea.

Ashera dismissed the feeling, tilting her head to the side. "You know what I am, then."

His eyes darkened further. "A monster of the deep."

Ashera grinned. Monster of the deep. She liked the sound of that.

In the center of the gardens, behind the manor, was a little pond full of fish. Sunlight made the surface glitter like a thousand stars. Ashera stared at the water, flashes of orange and yellow fins swirling about. She leaned over the pond, belly to the grass, and the fish darted away.

"I am a predator, after all," she said with a grin.

"Molly?"

Ashera clamped her mouth shut. She'd been so absorbed by the small body of water she hadn't heard his approach. She shifted into a sitting position, sapphire skirts pooling around her.

"You spoke," Clay said, disbelieving.

She tilted her head, staring at him innocently.

"Don't look at me like that." Clay strode forward and grabbed her arm, pulling her to him. "Speak."

She raised a brow.

"SPEAK!"

Spittle flung from his mouth, and she flinched.

"Your uncle is waiting in the drawing room, Master Burton." Finn walked toward them.

"Finally." Clay tightened his grip, and Ashera bit her tongue to keep from crying out. "Once my uncle gives his approval we will be wed, at which point you will speak two very simple words. *I. Do.*"

He released her and strode off without a second glance. Once Clay was well away, Finn closed the distance between them. "Your arm—"

"Do you have it?"

Finn pressed his mouth, then nodded.

"Tonight then. In your quarters?" she asked.

"Yes."

Ashera looked toward the manor. "Why does he need his uncle's approval? Why not just do as he wishes?"

"Clay's father left his uncle in charge of the estate and his finances. Clay must meet certain requirements listed in his father's will to inherit them." Finn held up a finger. "The first is that his uncle approves of his bride."

Ashera laughed. "His uncle will never approve. Perhaps he will release me yet."

Finn's eyes traced over her face, a bewildered look crossing his features. "Perhaps."

Finn's room was vastly smaller than her own, with only a few furnishings. Ashera sat on a creaky cot while Finn pulled over a small wooden chair and sat in front of her.

Ashera ran a finger along the cover of the aged book Finn had handed her moments before. Etched into the black leather binding was a woman with a fish tail in place of human legs. She looked fearsome, with dark hair that swirled about her head and long webbed fingers.

"You really did it. Did he suspect you?" she asked, hugging the book close.

"No, he was prowling about his rooms, breaking things like a caged beast. I believe his uncle did not give a favorable answer."

Ashera smirked. "I should have liked to see that."

Finn folded his arms over his chest, nodding toward the book. "Just curious. How did you ever expect to find the right book?"

"I hoped it would have pictures." She held it up, pointing to the engraving on the cover. "Like this."

"Fair," Finn conceded, "but how were you to understand its contents?"

"I was planning to force my maid. Slap her about a bit."

Finn snorted. "Slap her?" He shook his head, then said, "Liss can't read."

She tilted her head. "Why not? Can't all humans read?"

"Only the rich ones."

"Idiotic..." Ashera frowned. "Wait, you're not a rich human."

"I can read."

"Why?"

"My mother taught me."

"Was she a rich human?"

He took a deep breath. "No."

"Then—"

"There are some not-rich-humans who can read too, just not many."

"You should have specified then." She grumbled, picking at the black leather binding.

Finn sighed, rubbing the bridge of his nose. "Let's move on, shall we?"

"Fine." She shoved the book in his face. "Read it to me."

He held up his hands. "What? The whole thing?"

"Hmmmmm..." She sat back, noting the illustrations among the pages. She flipped through them, careful not to tear the paper in her haste. Nothing looked promising. She growled, turning them faster, until—

Ashera froze, then slowly turned back to the last page she'd flipped. In the illustration, a man stood before the ocean, a flute to his lips. She traced her finger over the flute, then down to the next illustration, where the same man stood over a mermaid that had been dragged onto the beach. In one hand was a knife, in the other a dark stone. The mermaid lay in the sand, blood leaking from a jagged wound in her chest.

She turned the open book toward Finn, shoving it into his face and pointing to the illustration. "This! Read this!"

Finn took the book from her, scanning over the pages. His brows knit together, eyes narrowing as he read. His jaw clenched tight, and she could see the muscle working there as his face paled. He cursed, setting the book in his lap to run a hand over his face before meeting her gaze, eyes haunted. "Did he really do this to you?"

Ashera lifted a hand to the buttons of her high collared gown, undoing them until the top of the fresh scar peeked out—thick, red, and rope-like.

Finn sucked in a breath, reaching across the space between them. A breath away from her skin, he stopped, fingers curling into a fist. "He cut out your…your…"

"My heart? Yes," she said, bitterness lacing each word. "Does it say how to get it back? The curse doesn't allow me to touch it, even if it is dangling right before me."

Finn let his hand fall, glancing between her and the book, then took in a long slow breath before turning the page.

"Does it tell you how?" Ashera asked when his silence stretched too long.

"It does."

Clay Burton woke to a low whisper in his ear.

"Where is it, Clay Burton?"

He groaned and flexed his hands, rope chafing his wrists. Breath hitched in his lungs, his lids flying open. He'd been bound to the bedposts by wrists and ankles, splayed out like an animal for slaughter. Above, a pair of large, deep green eyes arrested him. They were dark and alluring, framed by an otherworldly face that haunted him every moment. Silken ebony hair fell loose around her shoulders, wild as the day he'd first seen her.

Clay had found the flute and book among his father's things, the two wrapped in linens and stowed away in a chest. Intrigued, he'd gone to the sea and played the flute. He hadn't actually thought the lilting melody would reel in a finned temptress. But she had come, her emerald-green eyes peeking up from the water and stealing his breath.

So, he'd claimed her heart as his own and bound her to him and the surface.

"Molly," he breathed, forgetting his bonds. "Did you speak to me?"

"Where is the flute, Clay?"

Finally! Her voice was as hauntingly beautiful as he'd imagined. He strained against his bonds.

"Release me, Molly."

"Only if you release me."

Clay grit his teeth. Why did she not see reason? How could she want to go back to the ocean depths? Unthinkable. He'd saved her from obscurity, and soon she'd be his bride—

You will not wed some wretch you found from who knows where! Send her back to the streets or wherever it was you found her.

His uncle's words played through his mind.

No matter.

There were ways to be rid of those in his way. He pulled against the bonds, grunting with effort.

"Unbind me!"

"The flute, Clay."

Why did she keep asking for that thing? Why didn't she release him from these infernal bonds?

She straightened and held up a black, leather-bound book.

Clay felt the blood leech from his face. "Impossible."

She held up a knife and pressed it to his neck. "Tell me where it is."

"Never."

She pressed the knife harder.

"Kill me, and your heart will never belong to you again. You'll never be able to return to the sea."

13

A savage grin stretched across her face, her large eyes widening further.

Clay's breath froze in his chest.

"I would rather kill you and die here and now than be your bride," she whispered into his ear, pressing the blade farther into his flesh.

Warmth trickled down his throat. Blood. His blood. He could feel his heartbeat in his throat, each beat growing closer to the sharpened edge.

Clay's heart palpitated, sputtering in his chest like a dying candle flame. She would kill him. He could see it in the feral look in her eyes. "I-It's in the hearth. Within the wall on the left side."

She pulled away, wiping the blade on her skirts before going to the hearth. The flames had died out long ago—ashes cold.

"You hid it well," she said, before he could hear stone scraping against stone. "I would never have gone near the hearth. Disgusting, dry, sooty things."

"Molly, wait. You must see—"

"What must I see!" She returned to his bedside, the flute he'd played to coax her to the surface of the ocean held in a white knuckled grip. "That humans are foul, loathsome beasts that would tear out a heart with a grin on their face?"

Then, without warning, she snapped the flute in two.

The moment the flute broke, the barrier that had kept Ashera from reclaiming her heart shattered with it. And although speaking to Clay had felt like a betrayal to herself, standing with the remnants of her cage within her palm chased away any regret she might have had.

"Molly—"

"My name is not Molly, you feckless eel." Ashera didn't waste another moment, yanking the golden chain from his neck. The links snapped almost eagerly, a cool, heady oneness spreading over her as she cradled the sea green stone. Soft undulating light swept over the surface of the gem, like moonlight filtering through the ocean shallows.

It was time to go home.

Clay writhed. "No, you're mine. I caught you! I claimed you as my own."

Ashera ignored him, tossing the flute into the ashes of the stone hearth.

"I will find you," he growled, pulling against his bonds. "I swear it!"

Ashera smiled, raising the knife once more. "I think not."

Salt water caressed Ashera's feet. Ocean spray filled her lungs, and she tilted her head back. The scent of salt and scales washed over her, the song of her sisters calling from beyond the shallows. Stars filled the night, their iridescence like crushed abalone shells tossed across the sky.

"You can hear them, can't you?" Finn asked. His dark hair played about his face, swept up by the wind.

"I can." Ashera turned toward Finn. "What will you do now? Are you sure you won't avenge your master?"

He scowled. "Someone like him—" He shook his head. "Someone who could do what he did, deserved death."

"Our minds are one." She held up the stone—held up her heart— moonlight whispering over the smooth surface. "Thank you for bringing me back."

"Of course." He tucked an errant strand of hair behind her ear, fingers lingering a moment on her jaw.

The stone warmed in her hand. Something she'd never felt before.

"You should become a sailor," she said.

Finn laughed, and she decided she liked the sound. It was like music.

"Why?" he asked. "So you can sing me to my death?"

"Perhaps." Ashera bared her teeth in a beastly grin, and he laughed again, undeterred.

"Alright, maybe I will." His eyes softened, and he reached for her fingers, running his thumb along the back of her hand. "Until we meet again?"

"Until we meet again."

Ashera pulled her knife from the thin belt at her hip. and held it out to Finn.

"Make the cut."

He shook his head. "Ashera, I can't"

She took his hand and curled his fingers around the hilt. Their eyes locked. She would not plead with him. She would never admit that she was afraid. Afraid to part her flesh once more.

Ashera watched as he read the need from her gaze. Finn let out a slow breath before pressing his forehead to hers. The cut was swift and precise. It hurt, but the pain felt clean somehow, nothing like that day on the beach.

Her blood was hot against her skin, but that would change soon.

She pulled away from Finn and nodded to the knife.

"Keep it. Think of me when you use it."

He laughed, "You mean when I stab things?"

She grinned, then turned toward the horizon, the line between ocean and sky blurred by darkness. Asherah closed her eyes, walking out into the sea. Salt teased her tongue as she slid the stone beneath her flesh, the skin knitting up once more. Then, heart returned, she dove into the depths.

About the Author

Sara K. Anderson tends to acquire story ideas faster than she can write them down. When she isn't frantically typing words, she's listening to them; while washing dishes, at the gym or waiting to pick up her kids from school. Sara resides in Arizona where they claim two seasons—boiling hot summers, and mildly cold winters. Because of this, she and her husband love traveling to places with bright fall colors.

Sara will be releasing her debut novel *Fractured* in May of 2025 with a sequel the following year. Her other short story, "The Sea Witch and the Idiot Price," was published in the anthology *Creatures, Crowns and Curses.* If you liked this story and want to see more, follow her on Instagram @authorsara_anderson

Siren Songs and Syringes

by

Quiana Chase

Siren Songs and Syringes

The worst part about being a mermaid handler was that sometimes you had to kill the mermaids.

Peter Hampton tried not to think about what he was about to do as he removed his cochlear implants and filled a syringe with sodium pentobarbital. Or, as his younger colleagues referred to it, the "Forever Sleep Juice." The tank entrance was just a few yards away, and though Peter couldn't hear the massive pumps and filters anymore, their thrum still reverberated through his fingers when he touched the walls.

Today wasn't supposed to go like this. Both the girls had been perfectly amicable this morning—well, except for Kat. She had thrown her breakfast back at him, but that was par for the course with her.

Peter had learned by now that if Kat wanted to hit him, she could.

Kat had still gotten out of the water and crawled into her wheelchair, allowing her trainers to roll her out for her regular "meet-and-greet" with the aquarium patrons who sometimes threw rocks at her.

Someone had enjoyed her song a little too much. One incident of a kid trying to get into the mermaid enclosure was bothersome, but *seven* by the same individual stank of siren enthrallment, even if Kat hadn't ever become luminescent.

Mermaids were permitted in the aquarium. Sirens were not. Sirens meant death and lawsuits.

Maybe he could put this off for a little longer. Gemma still needed her medication, and it would probably be better to do that first. He wrapped a line of red tape around the syringe with the sodium pentobarbital, distinguishing it from Gemma's insulin, and set it in his lab coat pocket.

Retrieving Gemma's seaweed "treats" and insulin from the nearby locked closet, Peter approached the access area for the mermaid tank and let out a simple whistle. He assumed it made the same noise it always did, and half of a head instantly popped up from the water.

Cloudy orange eyes stared up at him, peeking out from a spreading fan of silky maroon hair.

"Not you, Kat," Peter said, shaking his head. Kat lifted the rest of her head from the water to bare her toothless mouth in what he assumed was a hiss.

Peter pointed at her. "Hey, no. Play nice." He signed at the other mermaids, but Kat couldn't see well enough. For her, he had to speak.

Kat brought up her thin, shark-like tail and violently splashed it against the water's surface. Peter leapt back, but the tiny wave still splattered against his boots. He made a face at her, and she stuck out her tongue before darting into the tank's depths.

The aquarium director cited Kat's "malicious behavior" as evidence she had turned into a siren, but the mermaid had always been like that. Sure, she was grumpy, but Peter would be grumpy too if his only hope for survival was living in a box.

Gemma, on the other hand, had been here since she was a baby, trapped in a fisherman's net and diagnosed with diabetes. She barely remembered the ocean.

Kat, though, was older than the United States. She hadn't forgotten.

Peter whistled again, carefully watching the water. A dark spot near the bottom of the tank squirmed upward, rapidly becoming larger and clearer until it leapt up at him with a massive spray of water.

He didn't even have time to offer a command before Gemma landed on the concrete outside of the tank, spinning wildly on her flat, scaly chest. Her webbed hands scrabbled across the floor in a futile attempt to slow herself down, and her momentum didn't stop until she crashed into the wall.

"You good?" Since he held Gemma's insulin, Peter said the words aloud. Gemma shook herself like a dog, brilliant blue hair and massive frilled tail whipping around, generating an additional shower of droplets. She pulled herself across the concrete with her hands, twisting her body around Peter's torso and peppering him with slimy, musty kisses.

"No," Peter said aloud, trying not to smile. "Down." He gently shoved Gemma's head away, and she relented, tilting her head and pressing her index finger into the inside of her bicep.

"*Shot?*" she asked with her hands. "*Shot? Shot? Treat? Shot? Treat?*"

"Yes." Peter swabbed her upper arm with disinfectant and injected the insulin. Gemma didn't even flinch; she'd been doing this twice a day for almost her entire life. The instant he pulled the syringe away from her skin, Gemma held out her hand expectantly and licked the chitinous scales lining her lips.

Peter placed a tiny square of dry seaweed into her webbed fingers, and Gemma popped it into her mouth without a moment's hesitation. She then made a single awkward sign with her hands.

"*Out?*"

Peter pinched his thumb and first two fingers together, shaking his head. "No."

The wide, rippling frills on the side of her head expanded and fluttered while she clumsily grabbed the air with both fists, thumbs extended up, rubbing the knuckles of her left hand down against those on her right. Her pronunciation wasn't perfect, but Peter understood what she was trying to say. "*Mean.*"

"*Yes,*" Peter said with his hands. "*I'm very mean. Go home.*"

Gemma made one more face and wriggled away, slinking backwards and headfirst into the tank with a gentle *plop.*

The other handlers were infinitely jealous of Peter's ability to communicate with his animals. Peter always told them they could talk with the dolphins and sea lions just as well if they taught them to use those buttons used by "talking" dogs on the internet, but that required a little too much work, and no one got paid enough as it was.

The time for procrastination was over.

Light flashed from the direction of the entrance, indicating someone had opened and closed the staff door.

Peter whipped around to see a kid bolt toward the water.

Shit.

"Hey!" Peter yelled, hoping his voice was loud enough to carry. "Stop!" He sprinted a few yards after her, trying not to slip on the wet concrete. The access area to the mermaid tank was massive, and maybe after today someone would actually take his complaints about it seriously.

The kid, maybe seventeen, did not turn around. Her eyes remained fixed on something in the water, and Peter risked a glance behind him to see Kat's head and shoulders rapidly approaching the edge of the tank.

Her mouth hung open in a song. It could have been a completely innocent vocalization. Maybe she wasn't trying to enthrall new victims. But considering a kid was trying to throw themself into a tank of magical fish monkeys, Peter was inclined to believe otherwise.

Picking up his pace, he lunged for the teenager and grabbed her ankle, grunting as his belly hit the concrete.

Kat locked eyes with Peter as she gripped the kid's shoulders and yanked her into the water, dragging them into the sapphire depths.

Peter was left holding a size seven Converse shoe.

He shouldn't have procrastinated taking care of Kat. Procedure demanded he contact the authorities immediately. Failure to do so would end in the termination of his job, assuming the siren didn't kill him first.

He only hesitated a moment before throwing aside his lab coat, kicking off his shoes, and diving in. The salt stung his eyes, but he forced them open, scanning the wandering cardinalfish and blennies for any sign of the kid or Kat.

There. A scarred shark tail twitched near the bottom of the tank, vanishing into one of the faux stone and coral caves. Peter pumped his arms and legs, praying the Mountainview High swim champion of '99 still lived somewhere in his bones. Pressure mounted behind his skull as he pushed through artificial kelp and maneuvered around the mast of a "sunken" pirate ship, keeping his gaze pinned to the depths below.

His lungs burned long before he even got to Kat's cave, and he realized he was probably going to die here. Kat would eat him, maybe—probably not. She didn't have enough teeth. She'd been an herbivore long before the aquarium rescued her from the beaches of California three years ago. But if she couldn't eat meat anymore, why had she turned into a flesh-devouring monster? Why had she specifically targeted a skinny teenager, and not someone…more… big…

Air. He needed air. No, he needed to rescue the kid, not convince himself Kat had done nothing wrong as she was trying to *drown a child*.

Peter reached the cave entrance as his lungs screamed. He groped at the lip of the rough, plastic rock and peered inside to see Kat's maroon form swirling around a figure in plaid flannel and denim.

Was the kid still alive? That's what it looked like. Kat hadn't even *tried* to eat her yet. She was just circling them with dizzying speed, incredibly close to the kid but never quite touching her. That was…good? In all his years working with mermaids, Peter hadn't seen one act like this unless they were protecting an egg.

All well and fine, except eggs could survive underwater for more than five minutes. Peter did his best to surge through the protective barrier Kat made with her body.

Before he could even reach her, Kat snapped out of her formation to headbutt his forehead, igniting fireworks behind his eyes and launching him out of the cave.

His head throbbed, and he kicked his legs again, determined to get right back in. Kat's mouth opened in a fierce hiss, and a tattered cobra collar lifted from her neck.

Great. She'd assessed him as a threat. Peter gritted his teeth and tried to gather the courage to take her down, but he noticed too late that her eyes were not fixed on him, but on something behind him. He turned around to see Gemma, her fine voluminous frills and tail writhing in a captivating display of cerulean and lavender.

Gemma opened her mouth in an aggressive grin, baring rows of teeth that elongated to needle-sharp points.

"*No!*" Peter signed as desperately and with as much exaggeration as he could. "*No! No! Stop!*"

If Gemma saw him, she didn't acknowledge it. Cyan light burst from her eyes, shattering her irises and leaving Peter blinded and disoriented. A deep hum vibrated through his bones, almost loud enough for him to hear, and thick nausea wrenched apart his gut.

Now he had to deal with *two* sirens.

Peter tried lunging for Gemma's wrist, but she twisted away as vibrant fluorescence rippled through the mottling on her torso and down her tail, transforming her entire frame into a neon flashing display.

Kat snarled, but didn't retreat, even though the illumination in Gemma's body coalesced into a sphere over her gut. As Peter frantically moved between them signed another warning, the sphere zipped up her torso, her throat, and exploded from her unhinged maw.

Gemma's blast hit Peter directly in the chest. His vision vanished in a blaze of white as he flew back into Kat's cave, spine *slamming* into the synthetic stone. He dropped to his hands and knees, limbs threatening to give out from beneath him as he coughed, gasping as cold air rushed into his lungs.

Wait.

Air?

One of the mermaids had made an air pocket for him. Trying to get to his feet, he grabbed at the cave wall, the grainy plastic slick with condensation. Salty snot dripped from his nose, and he swiped it away with his knuckles. A flicker of blue caught his attention, drawing his gaze to a blue tang flopping helplessly in the sand by his elbow. Peter scooped it up and gently tossed it at the cave's entrance, and it spun through the wall of water before flitting off to freedom.

He raised his head and stared into the face of a teenager with wide eyes and bleached hair plastered to her skull. She was trying to tell him something, but her enunciation wasn't great, and the poor lighting in the cave meant her lips were basically impossible to read.

"*-oo -ant let er -ie,*" the teenager said, pointing at the cave entrance.

Peter shook his head. "Can't hear you." He still followed her finger to see Gemma sink her teeth into Kat's shoulder, and the two mermaids rolled into a helix as they clawed and bit like fighting cats.

How was he supposed to get the kid to safety now? It was one thing to lift an Enthralled teenager through 300,000 gallons of water, and another to do it while two of the most dangerous creatures on Earth engaged in a fight to the death.

The kid screamed, face growing red. Peter helplessly tapped his ears. "I. Can't. Hear. You. Your lips are too hard to read."

Understanding lit up the teen's eyes, and she pushed her sopping flannel sleeves up past her elbows before attempting a very earnest, but slow, finger-spelling.

"F-R-I-E-T-D," the teen signed, pointing at the two sirens corkscrewing out of sight.

Frietd? That made no sense. Unless she mixed up her n and her t... Oh, she meant *friend.*

"They are not your friends," Peter said. "Especially not Kat. She's trying to drown you. We need to get you out."

The kid vigorously shook her head, sending water droplets flying across Peter's face. Aggression emanated from her fingers and her eyes as she signed again. "F-R-I-E-T-N-D." She caught her mistake this time, switching her thumb from between her index and middle finger to nestle beside her middle and ring fingers. "A-S-V-E."

26

"I will save you," Peter promised, though he wasn't sure how. He should have called 911 when he had the chance. At least then, there would be some help, though he didn't know of any police officers in Montana who specialized in siren attacks.

"N-O," the teenager signed, movements slow and halting as she likely struggled to remember the letters. "K-S-T." She pulled a rock from her pocket and pointed at a pile of very similar stones piled neatly in the corner. Kat stole things while on her excursions outside, and enormous efforts had been taken to keep her from bringing contaminants into the tank, including building more and more intense barriers between the mermaids and the patrons.

"She was trying to drown you," Peter said, folding his arms. "It doesn't matter how many rocks you give her, she's just going to—"

The kid took a deep, exaggerated breath, emphasizing the movement with her hands.

Maybe she had a point. They were still alive, which meant one of the mermaids—sirens—had made sure they survived. Maybe it had been Kat. Maybe Gemma. It didn't matter now. Either way, the kid wasn't acting like someone entranced by a siren, so hope was a possibility.

Peter took a deep breath and plunged his head outside of the cave, nearly overcome by the massive shift in pressure. He warily glanced around the corner to see Kat grab Gemma by the hair and repeatedly slam the glowing siren against the glass wall of the tank. He winced and pulled his head back inside.

"Take off your shoes, socks and flannel," he commanded. "If we want to save Kat, we need to get you to safety first." The kid hesitated, but ultimately obeyed, kicking off her one shoe.

"Can you swim?" Peter asked, miming with his arms. The teen nodded with confidence and pointed to a small tattoo of a surfboard on her forearm.

Okay, he could work with this. "Perfect. I will distract the sirens. You go up, lock yourself in the closet, and put on the headphones. Make sure they are turned on and playing white noise. Do you understand?"

Another nod, but Peter recognized the defiance burning in her pupils.

"If you want a chance to save Kat, you have to do *exactly* what I say," Peter said. "She could die. Do you promise to follow my instructions?"

The kid rolled her eyes and nodded yes again.

He still didn't believe her, but that was as good as it was going to get. Peter bounced on his feet a few times before jumping into the water wall, feeling like an anvil had been dropped on him. The kid followed suit and paddled up, moving with the grace of an experienced swimmer and the clarity of someone not entranced by a siren's song.

Why had Kat stopped enthralling her? Did Gemma's attacks force her to lose concentration on her song? As far as he knew, that wasn't how Enthrallment worked. Liberation only arrived in the form of death.

Peter remained puzzled as he maneuvered around the cave's corner, where Kat and Gemma still clashed against each other in vicious, sudden movements. He expected to see Kat glowing or manipulating some sort of siren magic, but her eyes and skin remained dull. A cloud of red billowed from the side of her head, where a chunk of her cobra collar was completely gone. Her advantage vanished as cyan light slowly built up in Gemma's body, and she clutched Kat's head with sharpened fingernails, widening her jaws.

Moving with a speed he hadn't achieved since his swim captain days, Peter crashed into Gemma and shoved his forearm between the siren's teeth. Gemma jerked back instead of biting down, tail lashing. Peter locked his arms around her before she could swim away, pinning her wrists to her torso.

Kat zipped away, a smoky red haze trailing behind her. Gemma squirmed in Peter's grip, but he managed to maintain his grasp as the glow faded from the flickering sections of Gemma's skin.

He didn't let go until he saw two bare feet disappear over the lip of the tank. Gemma lazily drifted away, entirely uninterested in either the kid or Kat.

The stupid fish just wanted to protect him. Stupid, *stupid* fish. Peter crouched against the floor of the tank and launched himself up to the surface, banging his elbow against the pirate mast.

With a gasp, he gripped the ladder and hauled himself out of the tank.

He would have felt relief, but the kid was hauling Kat's bloodied body out of the water.

"What are you doing?" Peter yelled, putting as much force into his voice as he could. The teen jumped, looking up at him with tears falling down her cheeks.

"Get to the quiet room," Peter said. "There is a siren—"

"I don't care!"

Even if he couldn't read lips, her words would have been sharp and clear.

"Please," Peter said, signing the word and speaking it. "You aren't safe."

"She was my friend," the teen said. Peter watched her lips carefully, and in the improved light, was better able to pick out what she said. "I met her in California. She just wanted rocks. No one let her keep her rocks."

Guilt wormed its way into Peter's stomach. He was the handler. He should have noticed how her mood was tied to those dumb pebbles. But he didn't, and now Kat was bleeding out on the concrete for a crime she'd never committed. Even as Gemma had torn her apart, she'd never transformed into a siren, never sung the forbidden songs. Peter had been ordered to kill an old, toothless mermaid who protected teenagers from misguided mermaid handlers and got grouchy when her things were stolen. And he'd been ready to do it.

He wanted to blame someone. Himself, the kid, the mermaids.

The supervisor who told him to kill the ugly and unpopular mermaid without a thorough investigation.

But there wasn't any room for that. Not now. Not when he had a job to do. He picked up his discarded lab coat, where the syringe of sodium pentobarbital still rested in the pocket.

When he looked up, the teen no longer cradled Kat's gently twitching body.

She stared into the tank, eyes glazed over, mouth twisted into a lazy smile as she shuffled toward water still cloudy with Kat's blood.

Peter brought his fingers to his mouth and whistled. Gemma appeared almost instantly, pulling herself out of the tank as light oscillated in dizzying patterns along her arms and tail. The teenager responded to the siren's every movement like a puppet with yanked strings, opening her arms and lips, likely matching Gemma's song.

"*Come*," Peter signed to Gemma. "*Shot. Treat.*"

Without a moment's hesitation, the siren flopped across the concrete and wound herself around him like she had a thousand times before, the thrums of a hypnotic melody pulsing from her throat. She nuzzled his face with her nose and playfully *thwipped* his cheek with her now-tattered frills.

"*Sorry*," Gemma signed, turning to Kat's lifeless form. "*Sorry. Mean.*"

She didn't react when he plunged the needle into her arm.

The worst part about being a mermaid handler was that sometimes you had to kill the mermaids.

About the Author

As a child, Quiana read the dictionary for fun and attended classes she was not enrolled in. This caused adults to assume she was not a troublemaker, so she often had success in rallying together fellow children to pursue outlandish and dangerous adventures. Sometimes involving wild bears.

Today, she has a much more reasonable head on her shoulders and channels her adventurous energy into writing, performing, and gaming. She is not currently active on social media, but there are not many writers named Quiana Chase, and if you type her name into the Amazon search bar you are likely to find a book published in February 2025. If not, her Magic the Gathering addiction got the best of her again.

Bet

by

Winona Morris

Bet

"*et misses you.*"

"*I know, Mamaw.*"

"*I miss you, too.*"

"*I know, Mamaw. I'll come for a visit soon, promise.*"

The call came around eight in the evening and Poppy almost ignored it. She had finally coaxed Donna, the adorable redhead from billing, to go out with her. Things were going great, and she was hoping for a second date, but nothing was a bigger turnoff than someone fiddling with their phones all night. She was going to ignore it, but she thought of Mamaw and the last time they had spoken.

"Sorry," she excused herself. "My grandmother has been sick. I should probably take this."

As far as she knew, Mamaw wasn't sick. She was an old woman, sure, but she was a strong and healthy old woman. She didn't know where that lie had come from, but as soon as it left her mouth, she knew it wasn't a lie. Mamaw hadn't said she'd been sick when they'd talked six weeks ago. Maybe longer. It might have been more like three months? Either way, by the time she had stepped into the restaurant lobby, she knew tragedy was on the other end of the line before she answered.

"Poppy, this is your Aunt Bootsie. You need to come home now. Your grandmother is asking for you."

She had run straight from the lobby to her car and was three hours away before she remembered she had ghosted Donna, leaving her sitting alone at the table and sticking her with the bill.

Tucker's Landing was a five-hour drive, and it was nearly two in the morning when Poppy arrived at the small clinic that served as the town's hospital if the ailment wasn't bad enough to be carried to the next city by ambulance.

During the day, the town, best described as quaint, looked like it belonged as the backdrop of a feel-good movie. There was one main street that was always decorated for whatever season it was. There were no corporate stores, just simple boutiques. The houses in the neighborhoods were small but well-kept. Nobody passing through would realize Tucker's Landing was inhabited only by independently wealthy families, or that the town had housed the same families for so many years that Poppy couldn't recall ever seeing someone from the outside move in, without marrying in.

It was a town built to give the rich the illusion that they were no different from the average person. It was a town full of hypocrisy that Poppy had fled from as soon as she could, with Mamaw's blessing.

In the earliest hours of the morning, it looked even more nondescript. Tucker's Landing could have been another unimportant wide space in the road, its streetlights barely lighting its existence. Only the clinic was lit, a beacon in the night.

Aunt Bootsie stood in front of the entry doors, a cigarette pinched forcefully between two fingers, glaring across the parking lot at her. The waiting room glowed yellow behind her, a promise of safety. Poppy could see Farrah, who she had gone to school with, sitting behind the reception desk. There would be a welcoming hug given by Farrah, but first, she had to make it beyond the most judgmental harpy.

When Poppy was close enough to see her aunt's expression, the woman took a deep drag of her cigarette and blew twin plumes of smoke out of her nose.

Aunt Bootsie reflected a younger Mamaw. She was short, with a soft round face and softer blue eyes. All that was missing were the laugh lines that crinkled when she smiled. Bootsie never smiled.

"You're late, you know. She died an hour ago."

Bootsie thumped the cigarette's butt into the manicured bushes beside the entryway. Poppy stared at the menacing glow of its ember and listened to Bootsie's heels, almost as sharp as her personality, clacking away into the dark.

Mamaw's house was on the outer edges of the town, where the river turned swampy and it often smelled like marshland. She was just as wealthy as most of the town, more than some even. She owned Brew For You, the little coffee shop in town. If people wanted to rent out the gazebo in the park, they had to come to her. Her annual donations helped keep the clinic, where she had died, afloat for some years. Her house was a little smaller than some, but just as well kept despite some people calling it, "that little shack beside the swamp."

The sun's light was just peeking over the horizon, painting the edges of the swamp pink, but the depths of it were still dark. Not far from shore floated a shadow that might have been a log but was probably a small gator.

Most everyone who lived in Tucker's Landing thought Little Deer Swamp was an eyesore, and the township probably would have voted to fill it in for more land but had been told multiple times by land developers that destroying the swamp would also damage their beloved river. It was easy for someone who didn't know their way around to get lost in its murky darkness. There were hazards of course, things typical to swamps like snakes and bugs and boggy areas hiding alligators. Some people even said it was haunted.

Poppy's favorite story had always been about the siren of the swamp. Some said that Little Deer Swamp, despite having no access to the ocean, was home to a mermaid. Some merchant sailor of an undetermined time ago had captured a mermaid while on the open seas and fallen in love with her. When he came home to Tucker's Landing, he couldn't bear to leave his beloved behind, so he brought her home with him and secreted her into the river. The mermaid, being angry at being taken away from the only life she had ever known, had turned bitter. She fled into the depths of Little Deer and hid from the sailor. The story went that when he realized she was hiding in the swamp, he went in after her, where she captured and drowned him. She continued to live in the swamp long after any mortal creature should have passed on, and she continued to drown any unsuspecting man who waded into her swamp. In some versions, the mermaid didn't drown men but would capture and eat anyone who blundered into her domain.

That one always made Mamaw laugh. "Nobody is living out there in the swamp besides Bet," she would say. "And Bet isn't eating anything we're not feeding her!"

There was no sign of Bet around now, and even if there were it was still too dark to see it, so Poppy found Mamaw's hide-a-key, under the same frog statue it had always waited under, and let herself back into her childhood.

Nothing had changed since she had last visited, and most of that was the same as it had been when she was a child. Memories of comfort and love flooded her, along with the knowledge that no more memories could ever be made with Mamaw. She had never felt so much love and so much misery at the same time before now.

The door opened into the kitchen. The small light over the stove was on, as it always had been, and lit the room well enough to see there was a note stuck to the old brown refrigerator with the glittery purple mermaid tail that had always been Poppy's favorite magnet.

She traced her finger over the scrawl of her grandmother's writing. The last thing she would ever write.

Bet is hungry. I am sorry.

"You should have told me, Mamaw," she whispered to the empty room.

They had found her at the edge of Little Deer, cold and unconscious, and nobody knew how long she had been there before someone found her.

Farrah, at the clinic, said it was a miracle that nothing had come out of the swamp and nibbled at her, even more so considering she was found curled protectively around a rotisserie chicken. Poppy knew it wasn't luck. Bet had been there, keeping Mamaw safe, just like Mamaw had always kept Bet safe.

Mamaw, lying forever still against the white sheet of the hospital bed, hadn't looked like she was sleeping. That was what people always said about the dead: "They look like they might wake up any minute." The body in front of her had been frail, bone thin, and sunken.

She had only woken up briefly after they found her. Just long enough to ask for Poppy.

"It was painless for her," Farrah said. "At the end, I mean. She just passed in her sleep. The rest of it..." Her old friend shrugged. "We all know cancer is a bitch."

Poppy chose not to go to the funeral. None of the family had reached out to her since Aunt Bootsie's dismissal at the clinic. She didn't want to subject herself to more familial snubbing by Bootsie and her current husband, Chad or Chet or whatever his name was. Cousin Mitzi would be there too, and that was a fiasco waiting to happen.

Mothers were not supposed to have favorites, but Poppy's mom had been Mamaw's favored child. "Bootsie was always too good for the rest of us," Mamaw said once. "Even in the crib."

Then Poppy's mom had died—cancer again, of course—and Mamaw took over raising her. If she hadn't already favored Poppy over Mitzi, she did once Poppy became her child as well as her grandchild.

Poppy and Mitzi spent a lot of time together, as cousins do, but Mitzi was a bully. She liked to pinch skin and pull hair whenever possible. She tried to frighten Poppy with scary stories, and when Poppy didn't get scared, she would push her down or threaten to hurt her. Her favorite thing to do was to wait until Mamaw was away and then tease Poppy mercilessly about how her mother had died and her father hadn't wanted her. She would say that the only person who ever loved Poppy was their senile old grandmother, who was so stupid that she had an invisible friend, like she was a toddler.

Mostly Poppy never tattled about the things that Mitzi said and did, but one day after her cousin had been particularly cruel, she cried into Mamaw's apron and said, "We should let her meet Bet! Then she would know you're not stupid. Then she would learn a lesson!"

Mamaw had just said that Mitzi and Bootsie should never meet Bet, that they would tell the rest of the town, and the town might force her out of the swamp, or, even worse, they might lock her away somewhere.

"Bet belongs to you and me," she said. "And you and me, we belong to Bet."

So while pretty much the entire town of Tucker's Landing gathered around the hole that housed the shell of the greatest woman she ever knew, Poppy threw a couple of frozen chickens from her freezer into a grocery sack and pulled on Mamaw's waders.

After pausing for a moment to see the spot Mamaw had been found, and noting how the grasses were pressed down around it, she went into Little Deer looking for her best friend.

"If you think I'm old," Mamaw said once, "Bet is much older. She was all grown up when we met, back when I was a tiny thing. She's always been there for me, but I worry about her. Nobody lives forever, and there's no way we'd get her to a doctor, is there?"

Poppy had giggled at the thought of loading Bet up into Mamaw's truck and taking her to the clinic. That would be a sight to see.

Now, she called out to her old friend. "Bet! Come on out now!"

The swamp, not used to sudden shouting, fell silent for a second. She strained to hear Bet answer, but there was nothing before the sounds started up again.

She checked the closest of Bet's favorite resting spots, but she wasn't there. It looked like she'd not even visited them recently. The chickens, though well on their way to thawing, were getting awful heavy, but Poppy pressed on. If Bet wasn't hanging out at any of her favorite spots, that meant she had holed herself up in her home. Probably mourning Mamaw. Not that anyone had been to tell her about her friend's passing. Bet just had a way of knowing such things.

Even Bet's home seemed empty as Poppy first came around the bend to where it was hidden. She felt her heart sinking. Something must be horribly wrong for Bet to not be in any of her usual spots, and not to come out to her calling.

Then suddenly she was there, rising up from behind some debris where she had blended in. Poppy scolded herself for staying away from the swamp so long that Bet's camouflage had fooled her. What if it had been a big bull gator instead of Bet?

Bet was terrifying enough.

She had pulled herself up to full height and was trying to puff herself up to look bigger. Her hair was a mess of knots entangled with leaves, twigs, and what looked to be the skeletons of a few fish. Her upper body towered over Poppy, and she swiped one of her clawed hands at the girl. Mud flew off her webbed fingers, spattering Poppy's face, but she didn't move to wipe it away. Behind her, Bet thrashed her large muscular tail in the water, trying to make enough noise to frighten away this unwanted intruder.

Bet hissed, a sound that oddly resembled a pot of boiling water, and opened her mouth as wide as she could, showing the promise of a death-dealing bite inside. Poppy could smell a stink of rot and sickness in the heat of her breath.

Bet is hungry, Mamaw's note had said, and that was the most understated way to describe the condition of her old friend. Bet was still immense, from the bottom of her torso to the top of her head she had to be almost six feet, and from where her pale skin turned into scaled armor, to the tip of her thrashing tail was almost that much again. The length had always suited her, but now it made her look too long for her body. Her skin was pale and thin. Usually a deep tan with a slight greenish tint, her flesh now looked sickly gray. Several bones in her shoulders and around her ribs pressed out so sharply they seemed about to rip through the skin. Her eyes, once the dark syrupy brown of the swamp's water, also looked gray, except for where the whites of them were yellow.

Mamaw had always been the one to take care of Bet. She fed her and groomed her. Mamaw's friendship had kept the wild creature docile. She'd tried to keep it up, even as the cancer had ravaged her body, as shown by the chicken she had with her as she began to leave this world. But as Mamaw had weakened, so had her care of Bet suffered.

Bet was intelligent, but was still a wild thing. Now she was a sick and starving wild thing, which made her unpredictable and dangerous. Worse of all, Poppy had been gone so long and visited so infrequently that she was practically a stranger. Bet didn't recognize her looks or the sound of her voice. Probably even her scent, surrounded so long by the city stench, was not the same as Bet remembered.

Bet swiped one more time before deciding that her feints were not enough to scare away this invader. Poppy watched her lower her body, tensing all the muscles she had. She saw the reptilian back legs, right where her tail disappeared into the water, digging into the sandy soil on the bank. She was about to lunge.

Poppy remembered the posture from her childhood. Mamaw used to bring Bet live food. A large sow bought from the fall fair, or a smallish herd of 3 or 4 goats. Once it had been a stag, one with a huge rack of antlers, but as tame as a child's pet. That one made Poppy a little sad, but she never asked Mamaw where she had gotten the tame deer from, because Bet had to eat. Sure, she would eat several pounds of raw meat, but she liked live prey the best. Mamaw would never let Poppy watch Bet eat, but would sometimes let her watch the hunt until the animal splashed so far into the swamp that it and its hunter were well out of sight.

For the first time in her life, Poppy was afraid of the siren of the swamp.

Poppy trudged her way out of the swamp what felt like hours later, though the glaring sun outside of the swamp's edges belied that. She was exhausted, splattered with mud and blood. Bet had gotten one good bite in before something had stopped her. Maybe it was her taste, or maybe just the smell had broken through the hunger. Actually, once Bet's teeth had sunk in, the mermaid had not only recoiled away but had shoved Poppy hard in the opposite direction. Poppy had landed on her back, smashing her head on the ground, which was surprisingly hard for the swampy area Bet had made her home.

By the time she had recovered some of her orientation from the head knock, Bet had torn open the bag with the chickens inside and devoured the birds. She had retreated to the water's edge and lay there staring at Poppy. It reminded Poppy of a cat, pretending to be a tame pet but unrelentingly predatory.

Even starving, Bet hadn't turned on Mamaw, but Poppy knew she wouldn't be extended the same courtesy. Maybe Bet had loved her once. Given enough time, she might love her again, but now, after having been gone so long, Poppy was just the food bringer who smelled similar to her old friend. A nearly tame animal might not bite the hand that feeds. But what if Bet hadn't been fed enough?

Getting herself back out of Little Deer had been harrowing. Bet had followed her all the way, moving when Poppy moved, stopping and staring unblinkingly at her when she stopped. Poppy hadn't felt safe until she was well beyond the water.

Trying to figure out how to explain the bite on her shoulder to Farrah at the clinic, and how to feed a 900-pound reptilian mermaid before it ate her, she almost missed the figure standing near the back porch of Mamaw's house.

The stance was exactly the same as what she had seen at the clinic when she first got back. Left arm holding right elbow, right hand pinching a cigarette that she thumps out on the lawn. It was almost enough to make her turn back into Little Deer and take her chances with Bet.

It was Mitzy this time, still wearing the slim black dress and heels that she had probably worn to the funeral.

"You look like shit," Mitzy said by way of a greeting.

Poppy stopped and closed her eyes.

"Did you really skip Mamaw's funeral to play in the swamp?"

"I was out there remembering Mamaw the way she'd want to be remembered. With her friend."

"Christ," Mitzy barked out a laugh. "When are you leaving?"

"I'm not," Poppy said and tried to push past her cousin into the house.

Mitzi grabbed her arm, and Poppy hissed in pain as it jarred the bite on her shoulder.

"What do you mean, you're not leaving? You have to leave. You've got to go back to your fancy job doing whatever it is that you do."

"I can work remotely," she said. "Hell, I can quit if I want to. We don't have to wait for the will to know that Mamaw left me the house. She left everything to me. I'm staying. I'm taking care of Tucker's Landing, I'm taking care of Little Deer, and I'm taking care of Bet. Who else is going to do it?"

Mitzi let go of Poppy's arm, not noticing the smear of blood that came off on her palm.

"You really are as crazy as the old bat was, aren't you? And who is Bet?" Her eyebrows raised as the answer occurred to her. "You're really going to stay here and be a thorn in my side to take care of a senile old woman's imaginary friend?"

This time Mitzi laughed until she was bent over and the laughter dissolved into a coughing fit. Poppy felt the old anger of her childhood. Mitzi had never loved Mamaw properly. Mitzi was always calling her mean things and hinting that she couldn't wait for her to die so she could get her hands on her part of the estate. As if there was ever a possibility of her getting any of it to begin with.

Then there was the fact that Mamaw never wanted Mitzi or Bootsie to find out about Bet, so how did she know, or suspect? Did that mean Mamaw had given up on her coming home, and turned to them for help?

"What on earth are you talking about?" Poppy asked as Mitzi recovered herself, wiping a dribble of fluid from her eyes.

"Mamaw started talking about her 'friend' all the time. She never said her name, just that she had a friend in the swamp that needed taking care of. Even kept trying to get us to promise to take care of her. Wouldn't get her to come to meet us, though. She couldn't because there wasn't anyone there, was there? The stupid old woman kept buying tons of meat to feed nothing and nobody. Probably tossing all those prime ribs to a gator or something."

Hatred flared up in Poppy stronger than it ever had before. She was angry at herself for not being there, for not coming when Mamaw had called her, but even more angry at her cousin. Mamaw never wanted to let anyone know about Bet, but in desperation at the end of her life had turned to the only family she had, and begged them for help. Family was supposed to help, but they just laughed, like Mitzi was laughing now. Mamaw was gone and in defense of her memory, Poppy said, "Bet isn't imaginary. She's lived in the swamp even since Mamaw was a kid. I've seen her plenty of times. She's waiting right at the edge of Little Deer for me to come back with a snack. She hasn't eaten properly since Mamaw got sick, apparently." Poppy put all of her bitterness into the last word, needling Mitzi as much as she could with the thought that she had neglected her grandmother.

Mitzi's eyes flicked to the tree line, then back to her cousin. "I just watched them lower my sweet grandmother into the ground. I'm not in the mood to go traipsing into the swamp."

"'Sweet grandmother?' You've just called her a crazy, senile old bat. The absolute least you can do is come down to the edge of the water and meet her best friend."

"Why can't you just bring her up here?"

Poppy shrugged. "Bet is a little eccentric. She's never left Little Deer in the whole time I've known her. She never even came to Mamaw's house. We always had to go to hers."

Mitzi looked out towards the treeline again, frowning at the marshy edges. "Okay," she finally said. "I'll go down there, just to prove that you're as crazy as she is. Nobody could live in that swamp, ever. And I'm not going any farther than the edge, so you can laugh at me ruining my shoes."

Poppy let herself fall behind and watched her cousin move away with long, defiant strides. She hoped Mitzi wouldn't decide to stop and turn around before she got close enough to the trees.

Mitzi had stopped moving and was facing the trees ahead of her when Poppy saw Bet start pulling herself from the water at the right.

When Mitzi's head snapped in that direction, Poppy knew she had noticed movement, and wished she could see the look on her cousin's face as she saw Bet for the first time.

Poppy looked at Bet herself, and tried to imagine what it might be like to see her for the first time. Right now, all Mitzi could see appeared to be a woman swimming freely in water that was home to alligators. This woman was naked, her crazy unkempt hair barely covering her breasts. She was tall and skinny, her ribs being painfully evident against the woman's skin.

Mitzi's head tilted to the side, and Poppy could see her jaw flex as she tried to work through what she was seeing.

By now she had to have realized that the coloring of the swamp woman was off. The gray-green shade of her skin must have been alarming. Also, she wasn't just tall. With her bottom half under water, her top half alone was as tall as any person Poppy had ever known.

To her credit, Mitzi didn't flinch when Bet started coming toward her. At least not until she made it to the bank.

While her skill in the water was unmatched, Bet's movements on land were not graceful. She dropped from her upright pose and leaned forward, using her hands as the forelegs she didn't possess. As she crawled forward, it reminded Poppy of an oversized baby, not yet sure how moving worked. Then her large crocodilian tail emerged from the water, and Mitzi took a step back.

Poppy had retreated almost all the way to the house. She watched, smiling, as Mitzi turned to look at her, eyes wide with fear

A bubbling sound, something like boiling water, made Mitzi turn her attention back to the swamp creature. With her back half completely out of the water, Bet had risen her torso again, towering over Mitzi. She opened her overly enormous mouth full of equally large teeth and puffed her emaciated body as large as she could, emitting the bubbling noise that Poppy knew was her version of a hiss. Bet was threatening her victim.

"I know you want the swamp, Mitzi!" Poppy called out. "Farrah told me all about it when I got here. While I was holding Mamaw's cold hand, she told me how you and your mother were standing over her dying body talking about a damned golf course!"

Mitzi shook her head violently back and forth in denial.

"You *knew* she was sick, the two of you. You knew, and you didn't make her get help. You didn't tell me because you knew I'd make her get help. You didn't want her to get help because you wanted her dead. You wanted her land. Well, bad news Mitzi, you can't have it. Neither can that backstabbing harpy you call a mother."

While Poppy talked, Bet continued crawling forward, awkward but silent. She was now within arm's length of Mitzi. Poppy knew her accusations were so distracting that the other woman hadn't noticed yet.

"Mamaw left me a note, you know," Poppy continued. "She left me a note and as soon as I read it, I had an idea. You know what that note said, Mitzi?"

Bet was now so close that Mitzi must have felt the heat of her breath run over her neck and smelt the rot of it. Poppy grinned a humorless grin when her cousin turned to find herself face-to-face with her grandmother's invisible friend.

"Bet. Is. Hungry." Poppy spit out each word.

Mitzi finally tried to run then, but the heels of her funeral shoes had sunk into the ground and she fell forward instead. Poppy watched as she tried to crawl away, looking more ungainly than even Bet did on land, but Bet had one clawed hand already wrapped around her ankle. With a quick yank Mitzi was pulled roughly backward, her short funeral dress rucking up around her shoulders. When Bet flipped her over onto her back, Poppy could see the smooth skin of her stomach exposed and slathered with mud.

The swamp woman crawled on top of Mitzi. Poppy could see flashes of the bright pink gills on the side of her neck as they pulsed with excitement. Bet opened her mouth again, dripping drool on the prone woman's face as she hissed, much louder this time, and finally Mitzy found her voice. The scream was shrill but cut off quickly as Bet sank her teeth into the woman's throat.

Bet began to feed.

Still smiling, Poppy retreated to the house. She had solved one problem, now she had a call to make.

Mamaw's phone sat in the same corner of the kitchen it always had, a groove worn in the floor nearby where she had paced as she talked. It was an old rotary phone, never replaced because somehow, against all odds, it still worked. As Poppy spun the dial, she heard a couple of loud cracks coming from the tree line. It sounded like Bet was dragging Mitzi into the forested part of the swamp instead of back into the water. She smiled even larger as someone picked up on the other end of the line.

"Aunt Bootsie," she said into the receiver. "You need to come out to Mamaw's place. Something has happened to Mitzi."

About the Author

Winona Morris always knew she wanted to be a writer when she grew up. When it became apparent that she was never going to grow up, she decided to become a writer anyway. After sharing her multi-genre fiction on various free blogs over the years she has finally decided to lock her imposter syndrome in a closet so she could be a "real" writer. Find more of her work in her collection *On Darkened Wings and Other Short Horrors*. She would love for you to connect with her on Facebook at https://www.facebook.com/winona.morris.author.

The Kindness of the Sea

by

Caitlin Barbera

The Kindness of the Sea

*H*enry met George and Farrars at a public house down by the waterfront. It wasn't the sort of place he would have taken friends to, in the old days, but it would serve them food and drink and give them a somewhat private corner table in which to speak about business, and that was all Henry really needed. He could be content with so little, at least for now. Soon enough, of course, his name would be on the lips of every worthy person of Charleston, of South Carolina. Perhaps of all the United States.

George swaggered into the public house like it was his own private room, of course, shouting Henry's name when he spotted him. It was as though they were still at school, in some hole in the wall in Columbia that students weren't meant to attend. Farrars was quieter, looking around with narrowed eyes before making his way to the table. Farrars had been Henry's father's man for years, seeing to the business of the plantation, and with the old man gone, he should have been Henry's man. That was how it would have been before the war.

Henry pushed the thought away and favored his friends with his brightest, most confident smile. "George, Farrars, it's good to see you. Please, order whatever you'd like. I'll be paying."

Farrars lifted an eyebrow. "That's good, Mister Courtenay. I'm glad to hear that. How is the plantation?"

Going to rot and seed, Henry thought, but didn't say. *Lifeless. Producing nothing, worth nothing.* He waved the question away. "It is much as it was, Farrars, unfortunately. It will need new investment to bring it back to its former glory. But I have a plan to get all that I need. That's why I've invited you here, to be my partners on a new venture."

George was already leaning forward, grinning. Henry could count on George, back in their college days, to be game for just about anything. Farrars would be the hard sell, he knew, but Farrars hadn't wanted to leave Ashley Woods. The plantation that had been in Henry's family for generations. If there was a way for Farrars to come back, for things to be as they were before the war, he would jump at the chance.

The war had upended everything, including Farrars' life.

"Tell me about this venture, sir," Farrars said, inclining his head politely. As if they were already back at the Woods. As if the fields were already humming with activity again, cotton being planted or harvested, wealth flowing into both of their pockets.

Henry smiled. It wouldn't take much, he thought, and then he would have Farrars. "I will need you to bear with me, I'm afraid, as this venture relates to my…peculiar fascination."

Farrars sat back, already looking disappointed, but George laughed uproariously and clapped his hands together. Henry had been prepared for this disrespectful reaction on both of their parts, and graciously refused to rise to the bait.

"Oh, dear, Henry," George said. "Don't tell me you've decided to actually go out on the water and search for a mermaid?"

Henry glanced around to make sure no one was listening to the conversation, then leaned in conspiratorially. "That's exactly what I intend. And I want you both to come with me."

Farrars shook his head. "Mister Courtenay, mermaids are just a story. The slaves must have heard sailors talking about them and spun their own stories about them. It's superstition, that's all."

George laughed again. "You won't convince Henry. He's had an encounter, after all."

Farrars cocked his head. "An encounter?"

Henry took a deep breath. "I don't believe you will have heard this story, Farrars. It was in college that I first confided it to others, friends. Like George here." Henry gestured toward him, and George gave a satisfied smile. He was the sort of man who always needed to feel as though he had friends, as though he was in the middle of all the important goings-on. "But it was when I was young. You recall the summer I nearly drowned, on Folly Beach?"

Farrars nodded and pressed his lips together. "You were in a bad way when you were finally dragged out of the water. I hope you're not intending me to believe in a dying child's visions?"

Henry frowned to himself. That was blunt. Far blunter than Farrars would ever have been with Henry's father. Well, there would be time enough to address and correct that sort of behavior. When

Henry had found what he was looking for, when he'd brought back proof of the existence of mermaids, when he was the talk of Charleston. There would be paid appearances, lectures, money pouring into his coffers. Enough to make Ashley Woods productive and beautiful again, just as it had been before the war. Enough to *make* Farrars respect him, like he had Henry's father.

"I would never have gotten back to the shore on my own," Henry pointed out. "I was far out to sea. Someone helped me." A beautiful woman, with the blackest hair he'd ever seen, that flowed around her like water weeds. Her eyes had been black, too, but her skin had been pale, looking almost as though it was shaded with blue. He didn't mention any of that, though, her beauty, the way she'd haunted his dreams afterward. He thought it would be counterproductive, and besides, if his information was correct, her true form was much different. "I might have believed, as you do, that it was merely a vision, but Sadie had seen it, too, when I reached shore again. She pulled me out of the surf and told me that a mermaid had saved me."

"Superstition," Farrars repeated, shaking his head.

"I'd known Sadie all my life, by that point," Henry countered. "She'd seen *something*, I could tell. She was utterly convinced of it."

Farrars, for his part, did not seem utterly convinced, but George looked intrigued. "What did she tell you about it when you questioned her afterward?"

Henry sighed. "Regrettably, I did not get the chance. By the time I'd recovered from the ordeal, she'd been sold away for her negligence, for allowing me to get so far out into the water. But her daughter remained at Ashley Woods. She didn't want to tell me, at first, all the stories her mother had told her, but I convinced her. She was the first to tell me that mermaids could shift their shape, appear like any creature of the sea."

"And you find that information reliable?" Farrars asked. Ever the practical man of business.

"Perhaps not if it was just one source, but it gave me a place to start. George can tell you how I've hunted up various accounts, tracked down the tales and the, shall we say, rules of engagement that appear again and again. I think I understand them better now, the mermaids. I think I am ready to encounter one, for more than just a brief moment. I intend to go out after them and bring back

53

one for study. I'll be famous, and you with me, if you decide to come." He sat back in his chair and gave them a practiced, fond smile. Let them think that there was some hope the expedition could go forward if they refused. Let them think he had options.

"You intend to just sail out with nothing but stories to guide you?" Farrars asked in a low voice, giving Henry a hard look. Farrars had frightened Henry when he'd been a boy, but Henry was a man now, and he held Farrars's gaze.

"Not just stories. You see, Farrars, I've found someone with first-hand knowledge. Someone who can lead us right to them."

The man had told Henry to call him John. He was an elderly black fellow, dark skin weathered from work in the sun, face lined and hair gone almost entirely white. He still walked with the upright bearing of a young man, though, and there was a certain lack of deference, as he made his way toward them down the docks, that Henry could tell Farrars and George had noticed, as well.

John carried only a small bag over one shoulder. He set it down on the deck when he was close enough to them to speak. "Gentlemen," he said, in a Carolina accent, and kept his head ducked and eyes down as he did. Henry relaxed slightly. "I'm here to show you where to find…the fish." He darted his gaze toward them and then away again, and Henry thought there was a flash of a smile on his face, there and gone so quickly that he could have imagined it.

"Where do you come from?" Farrars asked, narrowing his eyes suspiciously at John.

"Over near Hilton Head, sir," John answered. "My people were free from a long way back. Long before the war."

"Mister Courtenay tells us you have first-hand experience of these…fish we're looking for," Farrars continued, regarding the man with the same keen, narrow look he'd used to evaluate potential purchases at the Market.

"I do, sir," John answered. He kept his head lowered, but his voice was one of utter confidence.

Farrars turned and met Henry's eyes, jerking his head slightly before moving a few steps away. Henry followed, George in tow.

"I've heard one story of the mermaids," Farrars said in a low voice, glancing back at John, who stood exactly where he'd been before, looking out at the harbor. "Anyone who spends too much time around them goes mad. What makes you trust this man's account?"

"In my search for information, Farrars, I've become a rather good judge of character," Henry answered, annoyed at having to explain himself to someone who had once been in his family's service. "Anyway, if he's a madman, what can he do? We're taking a small boat, staying close in to shore. There are three of us and only one of him. Are you really afraid of him?"

The needling seemed to work. Farrars puffed up like an angered bird and huffed a breath. "Fine. But this is likely to end in a pointless sail and disappointment."

"Pointless? It'll be a lovely trip, at the very least," George put in jovially, clapping a hand to Henry's shoulder. Henry was glad to have George, and not just because the boat would take four men to sail it.

If only it were still the old days. He had never lacked for crew for one of his boats then. But crew was harder to keep when they asked for pay, and loyalty hadn't gone very far with the old servants of Ashley Woods. Not a one of them had come back, despite the fact it was their home; they'd gone where there was more money, probably to fall in with some beastly carpetbagger, and he'd had to sell off his boats one by one, until only the smallest was left.

He put all that out of his mind and stomped over to where John was waiting for them. "John here tells me it's four day's sail at most, there and back. I've laid on provisions for five, in case it takes some time to secure our specimen." He didn't think about how much of his remaining funds that had eaten into. It wouldn't matter when they'd found what they sought. "I see no reason to delay further. Let's get aboard. History awaits."

George whooped at that, but Farrars stayed silent, watching John. John merely picked up his bag and waited calmly to board until all the others had gone before him.

The first day of sailing went better than Henry's wildest expectations. He had sailed with Farrars before, and with George, but never with the two together; nevertheless, the three of them soon found a rhythm, working together to get the little boat underway, along the channel through Charleston Harbor and out toward the ocean. John, for his part, seemed to be everywhere he was needed, steady and quick at any task aboard the boat. Henry was impressed, in spite of himself.

At John's direction, they turned south out of the harbor, keeping the coast in sight as they traveled. They made good time. When night fell, they pulled in toward shore and tied up on a spit of sand. The lights of Charleston were far behind them, and Henry felt his heart soaring in his chest. He didn't even mind when Farrars turned a hostile look toward John that night, as they ate around a campfire, and asked, "As you're the expert, John, why don't you tell us a bit about mermaids that we don't already know?"

"Of course, sir," John said politely. "Whatever you say." He considered the question for a moment, the firelight playing on his face making him look as though he was smiling for a second before Henry could see his serious expression again. "Well, sir, one thing not many know is that the mermaids you see near the surface are all young."

"Young?" George asked.

"Yes, sir. They're *maids*, after all."

George laughed uproariously at that, but John's expression didn't change, remained just as serious and solemn.

"What happens to old mermaids, then?" Farrars pressed, and though he knew his companions believed not a word out of John's mouth, Henry still leaned forward, eager to hear the man's answer.

"Why, just the same thing that happens to maidens on land," John said. "They become mothers. Mermothers can't live near the surface, though. Only come up every so often to check on their kin. Then they go back to the deep, deep ocean."

There was a long silence, then George laughed again, and, to Henry's horror, Farrars joined him. "What nonsense!" George shouted, and Henry glared across the fire at John. Surely the man hadn't made up a story to humiliate Henry in front of his friends? That would be far too impertinent to allow.

But John's face remained solemn. "It's the truth. Perhaps one day you will see a mermother, and then you will know I told you only God's honest truth."

That quieted both George and Farrars, and they both glanced at Henry. In the dark, far from civilization, it was easier to believe in things like mermaids. Perhaps they were wondering if this expedition could succeed, after all.

They made even better time the next day. It was as though the winds and waves were conspiring to speed them along, and Henry couldn't keep himself from standing at the bow, the ocean breeze in his hair, and laughing with delight. George joined him, pleased as ever with a lark and a bit of time shipboard, but Henry could see Farrars glowering. Henry ignored him.

That night, when they made camp, John volunteered to catch them some fish for a fresh meal. While Henry, George, and Farrars built the fire, John took a fishing net that had been folded tightly in his pack and cast it out over the water. With the fire crackling merrily, Henry looked up to see John lifting the net, with two big, wriggling fish in it, out of the water, dipping it back in, and lifting it out again, over and over.

When John saw Henry looking, he smiled amiably and brought the net and the fish over. "Fear," he said by way of explanation. "It toughens the meat, but it sweetens the flavor."

Henry could see George and Farrars looking at each other uneasily out of the corner of his eye, so he quickly directed John to finish off the fish and get them cooking. When it was done, he decided John had been correct: the fish did taste far finer than any he had had before.

Henry brought out a bottle of wine to drink after dinner, of which he and George partook liberally, but both John and Farrars begged off. With the wine buzzing in his blood, filling his head with the wonder of what they would do the next day, Henry laid back in the sand, looking up at the stars, listening to George's snoring beside him. He rolled to his feet finally, only because he had to find a good place to piss.

When he returned to the campfire, he saw Farrars had rolled himself up in a blanket a little ways off, and George was still dead to the world, but John was sitting up, back to the fire, looking out at the sea. The flickering light of the dying fire made his shadow across the sand twist and dance, made his outlines hazy. Perhaps that was just the drink.

"John," Henry called to him. The man looked up and cocked his head in query, but said nothing. That was irritating, but not enough to spoil Henry's good mood. He beckoned to John. "Walk with me a moment."

John stood in a fluid motion that looked like it should have belonged to a much younger man, then loped to Henry's side. Instead of walking, they both stood together as the water lapped on the beach in front of them.

"Is there something you wanted to ask me?" John finally said into the darkness.

"Yes, I…" Henry hadn't realized it until he started speaking, but there was something. "Now that the others are asleep, I wanted to ask…" He looked sideways at John, who didn't return his stare. He didn't duck his head either, but held himself perfectly straight, looking at the water. "Tell me something about mermaids that no one else knows. No one but you." He had to know, he had to understand. The hunger was eating at his mind, the hunger to know everything.

"No one but you and me, of course, when I'm done," John said, voice low, and Henry nodded eagerly. "Fine. You know mermaids are shapeshifters?"

"They can appear as any creature of the sea," Henry said proudly.

John nodded, and there was another flicker of a smile on his face. "What I know that no one else knows is that it's not just creatures of the sea. They've learned to mimic the creatures of the land. They could be anywhere, as a bird, a deer, a dog…" He trailed off, and Henry couldn't speak, imagining encountering an animal in the stands of trees around the outskirts of Ashley Woods, only to find that the animal was a mermaid in disguise. It was so wonderful an idea that it took his breath away.

Perhaps, when he was the land's foremost expert on them, the mermaids would seek him out, come to his door to trade stories and knowledge. He wanted to weep with the beauty of the thought.

"Oh," he said simply, because there didn't seem to be anything else to say than that.

"You know a great deal already, Mister Courtenay," John continued. "Who taught you that mermaids are shapeshifters?"

"Oh, a girl, a house girl on my family's plantation," Henry answered, his mind only half on the conversation.

"Oh? What happened to her?"

"Hm, what? Oh, I don't know." Henry waved his hand as though waving the question away. "That's not important. I actually... When I was young, I... Well, I've seen a mermaid before." And before he could second-guess himself, he told John the same story he'd told George and Farrars two nights before. Had it really only been that long?

When he was done, John said nothing for a long moment, still gazing out at the water. "I see," he finally said.

"You don't believe me," Henry responded in a hushed voice. He didn't know why it should matter to him, but somehow it did.

"Oh, I believe you, Henry Courtenay," John said, and Henry was so overwhelmed by relief that he didn't even remark on John using his name like that. "Mermaids do save men or women who go out too far in the water. They like being owed. They always come to collect."

"That's fine," Henry said, a smile spreading over his face. "I would do just about anything to repay that mermaid who saved me."

John nodded as though he understood.

In the morning, when they boarded the boat again, John directed them farther out to sea, where the water was choppier. Farrars looked about to protest, so Henry cut him off. "I'm sure this boat can handle it," he said firmly, and busied himself about his work.

Farrars still caught his arm and leaned in, saying in a low, strained voice, "He is mad, Henry. Do you see? If that man John has ever encountered a mermaid, it drove him mad."

Henry yanked his arm out of Farrars' grip. "That's Mister Courtenay," he said coldly. "And mermaids need not always drive men mad. I've encountered one, after all."

For a moment, he thought Farrars was going to say something else, but he swallowed hard, a hint of strain showing on his face, and jerkily went back to his own work on deck. When Henry glanced toward the bow, he saw John watching them with a satisfied expression on his face.

Henry might have expected George to whoop and cheer as they set off, but his friend was as silent as Farrars, just staring out at their path with a fixed smile on his face and wide eyes. That was good, Henry thought; the quieter they were, the less chance they would frighten away their quarry.

They were so close now. So close to the moment he had been waiting all his life for. A trickle of apprehension flowed through his brain as they left the land farther and farther behind, but he pushed it out of his mind. Once he found the mermaids, everything would be alright. He could hire workers, restore Ashley Woods to its proper glory. It would be as though the war had never come along to spoil everything. He could be so much more than what he was, if he just found them.

John wasn't helping them sail the ship anymore. He was merely standing in the bow, looking out at the sea. He didn't seem to need to hold on to anything to keep himself steady; no matter how the boat tossed and bucked on the larger waves, he stood straight and tall.

And then George gave a cry, echoed a moment later by Farrars. Henry wrenched his gaze away from John's back and to the water where his friends were looking. There was something enormous down there, coming up from below, a terrible dark shadow that was coming steadily closer, undulating through the water like a nightmare manifesting in the waking world.

Henry couldn't move as he watched it. It seemed that George and Farrars couldn't, either.

"John," Henry choked out. "John, what is that?"

He watched out of the corner of his eye, frozen, as John ambled over, not seeming to be affected by the *thing* coming closer. "Why, it's a mermother, of course. I told you they do come up now and again to check on their daughters. And dutiful daughters bring them tender morsels to feast upon."

John's voice didn't sound right. It didn't sound like it had before, cracked and raspy from a lifetime of hard work. Henry turned his head with a great effort to look at him full on.

How had he thought that John looked old? He'd thought the man weather-beaten, but there were no lines on his face now. His skin was utterly smooth, practically luminous, his body thick with muscle, his hair extending past his shoulders and rippling in the breeze as though it was lighter than air. When the light shifted, it shifted the color of his skin, too, black as a fish's eye to pale as a fish's belly, always with the suggestion of blue beneath whatever color he seemed.

"You... You," Henry started, but couldn't finish.

"I did warn you," John continued. "I told you that mermaids could appear as beasts of the land. And I told you that the mermaid who saved you would come to collect on what you owed."

"It was you," Henry said, wonder filling his voice. "You're the one..."

He—she—*it* grinned, and there were so very many sharp teeth in its mouth. "So I did."

"Why?" Henry asked desperately, the question that had been tumbling through his mind for years. "Why did you save me? What is my purpose, my destiny, that you saved me for?"

The mermaid threw back its head and laughed. "Purpose? There was never any purpose. It amused me. And now it amuses me to take your life back, for my mother." It gestured toward the sea, where the shape had grown tremendous as it grew closer. It was human-like in only the vaguest sense of the word, its fishlike movements looking impossible and nauseating. "Nothing kind ever came from the sea, Henry Courtenay," the mermaid continued. "You are a cruel man, so you should understand."

"What?" Henry asked, bewildered and hurt. "I'm not a cruel man. I'm a good man, a decent man."

The mermaid simply laughed again, then leaped up and arced its back so that it sailed over the side of the boat and dove into the water with barely a splash.

In the next moment, the *thing* coming from the depths struck the bottom of the boat, and Henry found himself plunged into the cold, churning sea. When he broke the surface, he could hear George and Farrars screaming; those screams cut off abruptly, and it was only him and the sound of the water.

And the shadow moving below him. He looked out and glimpsed his own mermaid, his childhood savior, watching him with a smile he recognized from the docks, from the campfire at night, the one that had been gone so quickly he hadn't been sure of its existence.

Its head disappeared below the waves, and he was alone with his death. For a moment, an eye so black and wide that it might have been the void itself peered at him. Then there was nothing but a mouth that filled the world.

And then there was nothing at all.

About the Author

Caitlin Barbera is a lifelong lover of reading and writing science fiction and fantasy. Her first story was about a girl velociraptor going on an adventure and fighting androids. She is currently a student in the Genre Fiction concentration of the Graduate Program in Creative Writing at Western Colorado University. A native of Colorado, she currently lives in the Denver metro area with her spouse, child, and dog, and spends much of her time coming up with more story ideas than she could possibly write in a lifetime. She can be found at caitlinbarberawrites.wordpress.com.

Superior's Corpse to Water Ratio

by

A. M. Symes

Superior's Corpse to Water Ratio

elly didn't usually sing out loud while working, but Sugarhill Gang was speaking straight to her soul that morning and she just couldn't help it. She got halfway down the hallway of the lower-level interior cabins when a lobster-red man, in boxers he only wished he could fit into, erupted from his interior cabin room and shouted down the hallway after her.

"It's six in the morning! We're trying to sleep!"

Kelly continued singing, refusing to hear Lobster Man over the music blasting from her headphones. She was finding it increasingly difficult to distinguish the real guests from the...*not* real guests...so she ignored them all. She kept singing while pushing her cleaning cart down the corridor, pretending not to hear other guests in other cabins shouting for her to quiet down.

They were on day thirteen of a fifteen-day Great Lakes cruise, the only day the ship was entirely "out at sea" as they headed away from Toronto, Ontario to Duluth, Minnesota, skirting through the center of Lake Superior. Kelly planned to work the interior cabins until sunset when she'd clean the balcony cabins while pretending she could see land through the darkness.

She surprised her family when she gave up her maid job at the motel in town for a cruise ship job, considering her fear of open water, but she justified the move with the much higher paycheck. Plus, most cruises had very few days completely out to sea, and she argued the Great Lakes cruises were not really out to sea since the lakes are landlocked.

Kelly paused as she passed a small window in the corridor and took a moment to look outside. The sun had not risen yet so her view was mostly darkness. But when she squinted, she could see winking lights from homes along the shoreline. Land was close by.

The real reason Kelly had to get away from her motel job was the ghosts in the swimming pool. The one perk to working at the motel was use of the big swimming pool, something Kelly's friends and family took advantage of frequently. But they couldn't see the others already in the pool. Some were swimming and tanning in the lounge chairs as if they were regular—albeit semi-transparent—motel guests. But most were in varying degrees of decomposition and "living" an endless loop of their final horrific moments alive. Watching a ghost sink to the bottom of the pool wasn't so bad. Sadly, Kelly had seen that scene play out so often that she was used to it. What burned into her mind was the dead people who spent agonizing minutes silently gargling water and blood, frantically flailing for help that would not come, until they faded away into the blue water...only to reappear and start the process all over again.

There was nothing sinister about the particular motel Kelly had worked at that caused so many ghosts. Every motel, hotel, and resort Kelly visited had a steady flow of living and living-impaired souls streaking through the pools. People drown a lot. And some people really love swimming, so they hang around after expiring to enjoy the afterlife poolside.

Despite her friends and family partaking, Kelly never swam. They all assumed it was because of her father. He had drowned after his fishing ship sank outside of Manitowoc, Wisconsin in Lake Michigan, when Kelly was thirteen. In the *Great Lakes Bermuda Triangle,* the bullies in the neighborhood teased, but her mom assured her the ship sank before crossing the haunted barrier. Kelly wasn't sure she believed her mom, especially since there were no storms, no swells, no other boats in the area when her dad's ship sank. And there was never any evidence recovered; the ship and her dad were on radar and with one blip, they were gone.

Her dad disappearing may have been part of the reason Kelly didn't like water. But the real reason was the corpse to water ratio.

People will swim in the Great Lakes and the oceans and the rivers, even though there are many corpses in those bodies of water. People will not swim in a pool with a corpse in it, though. Humans all have a corpse to water ratio that is acceptable for them to swim in. And Kelly had a strict corpse to water ratio acceptable for her to swim in: zero to one.

When she took the cruise job, Kelly incorrectly assumed a ship would have few—if any—ghosts. And if there were spectral guests, the continuous movement of people getting on and off at ports meant Kelly could disregard the real and not real bodies equally.

Except on sea days. Staff, guests, and ghosts were trapped aboard on sea days.

Kelly continued down the long corridor, then halted when she spotted a young girl in a swimsuit with flippers on both her feet and goggles that looked much too big for her.

"You're up early, sweetpea," Kelly said, taking her headphones off. "The pool doesn't open until 8:00 a.m."

The little girl tilted her head and smiled at Kelly.

"And it's on the upper deck, not down here, silly," Kelly continued. Adults could be horrible, but kids always brought a smile to Kelly's face. They were so innocent and just wanted to have fun. *We could all live that way,* Kelly thought.

The little girl continued to smile and tilt her head. Farther. And farther. When her ear squished into her shoulder, Kelly finally realized she was not talking to a real girl. The girl's neck cracked and popped as her spine unhinged to allow her to keep tilting her head. The skin along her neck tore—in a soft *plop* as if it were silly putty stretched too far—and her head dropped into her waiting hands. Kelly tried not to throw up her breakfast as the little girl tossed her own head up and down a few times, like a game of basketball.

"Sweetpea, please leave me alone," Kelly whispered.

The headless body took an awkward step forward, flopping a flipper down hard on the floor. The little girl's eyes were fixed on Kelly, although her head was upside down so her eyes looked a little buggy.

"Please don't," Kelly started, then screamed when the little girl wound up and pitched her own head straight at Kelly.

Dropping to the ground and tucking into a ball, Kelly anticipated the squelch of a child's decomposing head landing on her.

"For crying out loud!"

Kelly poked her head out from her arms and saw the Lobster Man, his beady little red face staring down at her.

"I paid good money for my girlfriend and I to have a nice vacation. We don't need to listen to you sing and scream like a bag of dying cats!"

Kelly looked around and the little girl was gone, but her head was sitting on the cleaning cart between the fresh towels and face cloths.

When the head started singing, "Row, row, row your boat, gently down the stream," Kelly grabbed her headphones and jammed them to her ears and pressed play, bringing Sugarhill Gang back to life.

"Hello? Are you even listening to me?" the man yelled.

"Honey, it's not fair to judge her. You're spoiled by my lovely songs every morning," a sing-song voice came from behind the man. "Plus, I don't think she's all there."

A woman with thick black hair tousled around her head appeared and grabbed the man's arm, twirling a finger around her ear to gesture *crazy*, then smiled at Kelly.

The man seemed to slip into a romantic trance as the woman cooed in his ear. She whispered something to him, and he giggled, then he turned his puppy-dog smile towards Kelly and asked for a fresh towel. Kelly grabbed the tip of the towel the ghost head was sitting on, then whipped it fast so she didn't accidentally touch the little girl's stringy hair. The towel snapped against the man's bare stomach as the head flung off down the hallway.

"Are you serious?" the man shouted, his face snapping back to angry red, but Kelly was already running in the opposite direction with her cart before the little girl could come back to retrieve her missing head.

Oddly enough, when she really needed to figure out the difference between the real and not real people, Kelly judged them by how kind they were. Ghosts usually knew they were not supposed to be there, so they stuck to the shadows and nooks and crannies and were, for the most part, polite. The air-sucking people felt they deserved extra attention because they paid good money to be there. They walked down the center of the hallway, refused to move out of the way, were belligerent, and demanded services.

Lobster Man and his girlfriend with the gorgeous hair were real people. The three people standing in three open cabin doorways, watching as Kelly ran by, may or may not have been real. They seemed real, but they were also sticking to the shadows of their rooms. But the giggling noise that Kelly could hear, despite her rap music blasting in her headphones? That was not from a real person.

Once out in the sunshine of the top deck, Kelly sat down by the closed pool. She reclined in one of the chairs and closed her eyes, feeling the warmth of the rising sun with the brisk sea air. She removed her headphones and took a deep breath to lower her heart rate before her heart burst from her chest. The ghosts didn't always scare her, but something was particularly disturbing about the little girl's giggles that set Kelly's nerves on fire. With her eyes closed, she could pretend she was on the beach with her mom, just another day.

It was quite early in the morning, guests all sleeping and the crew busy below deck preparing breakfast and morning activities. Since this was the maiden voyage of *The Phantom Paradise*, Kelly had hoped to avoid ghosts. At least the pool was quiet; no splashing of bodies. The little girl ghost was most likely a stowaway from their last port in Sault Sainte Marie, Michigan, or she was haunting a family onboard. Kelly didn't know the rules of being a ghost. Not a single person alive knew what she could see except her priest, but even he believed she was cured. After her seventh intensive prayer session with him, when she realized the ghosts were not leaving, she told him she didn't see the ghosts anymore, then hoped lying to a priest wasn't too big of a sin.

"It's beautiful, isn't it?" A voice interrupted her peace.

She opened her eyes and Lobster Man's girlfriend was standing at the bow, staring directly into the rising sun. Her body was perfectly outlined in the sunlight, making her appear to glow. Her floor-length, green cotton dress and thick black hair swirled around as if she were swimming slowly in circles underwater. If Kelly hadn't seen her a few minutes ago, she would swear she was looking at an angel.

Kelly got up and joined the woman at the bow, gripping the handrailing tight. She wouldn't fall, she knew that. But she was terrified nonetheless, of plummeting off the edge of the ship and crashing into the lake, where she could sink through the crushing dark water…

"Isn't it beautiful?" the woman asked again.

"Yes," Kelly replied.

She lifted her eyes and stared at the sun as it rose along the water. It wasn't as yellow as she expected, but an almost burnt orange. Orange like fall leaves. But it was beautiful, and as the light sparkled along the calm water, Kelly wondered if it wasn't so bad being out to sea. There was no land to block her view, no cities or boats to cloud the expansive blue water. And despite the sheer number of bodies in the Great Lakes, Kelly had yet to see one on the surface as, she assumed, they were all on the bottom.

"It really is beautiful," Kelly continued. "I haven't really look at the sunrise, or the water. I guess I should look more."

"Orange at night, sailors delight. Orange at morn, sailors take warn," the woman sang. "Bad omen for you, sweetpea."

Kelly's dad used to say that before sailing out. She twisted to look at the woman and started when she found her much closer and staring directly into her eyes. When Kelly tried to take a step back, the woman grabbed her arms and dug her long, sharp nails into Kelly's flesh. The woman's eyes were not kind like her voice. Her eyes were deep pools, as black as her hair.

"I wasn't talking about the sun being beautiful," the woman growled. "I was talking about the black depths just below your feet, just below the surface of this ship you think you're safe on."

Kelly squirmed but could not get away.

"What are you doing?" Kelly asked, her brain telling her this was another ghost and an evil one at that. How could she miss that this woman wasn't real?

"I assure you I am real," the woman said, answering Kelly's thoughts. "Evil? Well, that's a matter of perception, sweetpea. I'm charged with feeding the creatures below, sustaining their peace, which, in turn, keeps this beautiful water planet of ours at peace."

Kelly's head swirled. She didn't like where the conversation was going, but she could not break the woman's grasp no matter what she tried. She thought of screaming for help but assumed she would be tossed overboard if she did that.

Where is that little girl? Maybe she can help! Kelly thought as she tried again to yank her arms free.

The woman smiled, her lips parting wide, and Kelly was smothered with the pungent smell of decaying fish. The woman's teeth were not human, but rows of razor-sharp needles.

"Don't eat me!" Kelly cried, going limp at the thought of those teeth ripping her flesh from her skeleton. Her imagination took over with visions of teeth shredding her skin and blood pouring down the side of the ship filled her mind.

"I'm not going to eat you. Lobster Man—I like that nickname, by the way, it's clever. Lobster Man will be my meal. You are for someone else."

The woman wrapped her arms around Kelly's waist in a strong embrace. A rush of helplessness swam through Kelly's body, as if her veins were contaminated with slimy eels, a sinking, surging tide of chaos that paralyzed her. Despite the warmth from the woman's body pressing against her, Kelly trembled. Her face quickly drowned in a sea of black hair as the woman bent forward and kissed her, softly at first, and then with a swift intensity that made Kelly grab the woman's arms to prevent herself from collapsing. The only steady thing was the woman's gaze, locked on Kelly, keeping her from spinning out of control with the situation. She tried to clench her lips tight, but the woman worked a slippery tongue between them, and before Kelly knew it, the woman's tongue was twisting around her own. The woman locked her lips tight around Kelly's and inhaled deeply, sucking the air from Kelly's lungs in an awful drag.

And as quickly as the woman had sunk her soft lips into Kelly's, she pulled back, tongue retreating, and the last thing Kelly heard as she fell backwards, flipping over the railing, was the woman singing, "I hope your flesh tastes as good as that kiss."

The impact of hitting a calm water surface from the height of the top balcony of the ship should have killed Kelly. And she wished it had as she sank below the surface, quickly losing visibility as the early morning sunrays faded. Kelly wasn't able to take a breath after the kiss, and she knew she was seconds away from the awful convulsions that accompany drowning. She'd seen too many people—well, ghosts—drown in her lifetime, and despite not experiencing it herself, it looked like a terrifying and painful way to die.

The pressure building around her body was the most intense physical feeling she'd ever had, but it didn't crush her. Kelly knew she was panicking, and panic distorts time, but she also knew she should have died quickly. She wasn't sure which would be worse: her skull collapsing from the pressure of the water weight or the pain of inhaling the icy liquid when her body finally overrode her willpower not to breathe. Crushing pressure seemed worse, so she fought her own mind and opened her mouth to take a breath of water.

Her lungs burned as water filled them, and Kelly coughed painfully. Then she took another breath of water. And another. Each breath burned more painfully than the last, but she was not dead.

How am I alive! she screamed into the blackness.

The concept of space and direction was gone. She had equal feelings of free falling from the balcony and being sucked underwater. The logical answer was she was sinking, but how fast or slow she didn't know. The chest-squeezing breaths continued to fill her lungs with water.

She kicked her feet, flailed her arms, but she continued to sink.

And then she wondered if she was already a ghost.

She stopped breathing, and nothing changed.

The panic evaporated into terror, and she swore her body sank faster into the nothingness.

Is this what Dad felt when his ship went down?

Twice she felt like something swam past her, spinning her around like a whirlpool. The woman's song—*orange at night, sailors delight*—filled her mind. And at some point, she bumped into a massive object. There was no light to see what it was she hit, and she only believed it was massive because of the pressure change she felt as she slipped by. She reached a hand out and felt a spongy surface before she fell off the side of whatever it was to continue her descent. She thought everything living in the Great Lakes was small, but this was much bigger than her. And alive, since she felt a swirling current as it swam away after her touch. Then again, Kelly also had thought mermaids were not real, but that woman on the cruise ship had to be something like a mermaid, with that hair and those teeth.

The captain of the last ship Kelly worked on had told her that the area of Lake Superior where the cruise ships passed was only five hundred feet deep. Deep enough to drown, yes, but how long did it take a body to sink five hundred feet? Still unsure if she was a ghost, or if she was alive by some evil magic from the woman's kiss, Kelly continued to kick her feet and flail her arms. Every few minutes she thought she could see the outline of something, maybe a light, but then everything was black again, and her eyes strained to find anything to lock on to.

At one point, a small mass came towards her, this one with a pinprick of a light, and she remembered fish in the deeper parts of the ocean could light up. Maybe some fish in Lake Superior can light up, too? The light got closer, and she put her hand out. A sharp fin cut her and the light disappeared before she could pull her hand to her chest to cradle it. She hoped she was bleeding and the blood would attract something that would eat her and get the torture over with.

And that's when she crunched into the ground.

She sat awkwardly, like trying to sit at the bottom of a pool. Testing if it was actually the bottom of the lake versus another sea monster, Kelly kicked at the ground. It was sandy and solid. She stood and tried to push off.

Maybe swim to the surface, she thought, but the water rushed by as if she wasn't moving.

Then a hand reached out and grabbed hers.

She silently screamed, no bubbles coming out as there was no air left in her, but the sound ricocheted through her mind. The hand tightened its grip on her wrist, and she tried to pull away but could not move. Kelly feared it was the woman again, but this hand felt soft and spongy. *Waterlogged.* She couldn't bring herself to reach out to feel what was at the end of the hand, her body frozen in another depth of fear she did not know a person could survive.

A glimmer shone above. Tracking its sporadic movement, Kelly thought it must be another light-up fish. She willed it to come her way, to light up the area she was in so she could see what had taken hold of her. The light danced closer, then away, then closer, jumping around in a way Kelly pictured a fish swirling down a drain. She didn't think her heart was actually beating anymore, but if it was, it felt like it was three beats away from breaking out of her ribs.

One.

Two.

Three.

The fish dropped lower, illuminating the white sand on the lake floor. And spread as far as Kelly could see in every direction were people. Corpses. In varying states of decay and bloating. All with nibbles, bites, chunks of flesh removed, leaving behind jagged holes for water and small fish to swim through.

I've broken my corpse to water ratio rule, she thought, then wondered if tears were actually flowing from her eyes, because the burning sensation felt like tears.

As she pivoted, the corpses followed her movement. They were watching her, their eyes following her. She'd seen plenty of dead eyes, but the faces looking back at her were not dead. They were somehow still alive, or not completely dead. Then she sucked in a lungful of water as she recognized one body a few feet to her left.

It was Lobster Man. His face was contorted in sheer pain and when Kelly dropped her eyes, she knew why. A gaping hole was gnawed through his stomach, just above his tiny lobster shorts. And flowing through the hole was beautiful black hair.

"I forgot to mention," the woman sang, her voice no longer sounding like a whimsical song but instead like screeching, raw vocal cords. "They like their meals fresh."

The woman's floor-length dress was now the shape of a large fin, which was curled around Lobster Man's legs to keep her steady as she shoved her head into his stomach cavity and tore off another bite of flesh. He silently screamed.

The hand gripping Kelly tugged at her slightly. Turning back to what was in front of her, Kelly had a flash of her father through her mind.

Maybe it will be him. We will spend eternity together.

It was just a flash of hope, but enough to elevate her spirit a fraction before she came face to face with the little girl with the flippers. Her head was floating a few inches above her body to be eye-to-eye with Kelly.

The head began to smile just as the light fish swam away, plunging Kelly and the sea of corpses into darkness.

About the Author

Camping as a child, the adults use to tell this author that the yipping noises in the dark were from banshees hunting for kids up past bedtime. She still believes banshees are lurking in that dark line at the edge of campfire light and enjoys bringing readers to the edge of the light to make them squirm. A.M. Symes writes suspenseful, ghost-infused stories, some of which have infiltrated publications such as Crystal Lake Entertainment, Sirens Call Publications, Creepy Podcast, Tales to Terrify, and NoSleep Podcast. Symes lives in Minnesota with her best friend and a banshee.

If you enjoyed this creepy tale, feel free to follow Symes and her horror chatter on amsymes.wordpress.com.

Sea Monkeys

by

Marella Sands

Sea Monkeys

I want one!"

I glanced over to see what had attracted the attention of my youngest hatchling. His tailfins shivered with excitement, and he pointed at a rather large air bubble inside the pet shop. The sign over the bubble read *Sea Monkeys*.

It was difficult to see into the bubble from outside the shop, but I'd seen sea monkeys before. They were a waste of resources: delicate and difficult to keep. A better pet would be a reef fish. Even a freshwater fish, which would require special salt-free water, was easier to keep than a land animal.

"I don't think so," I said. "They don't live long under the sea."

"But they have air," said the hatchling. "I could keep it in air, couldn't I?"

"Air goes bad fast," I said. "It takes a lot of work to keep the air fresh enough for them."

"I'd do the work!"

I'd heard that before. Of course, it had then been me begging my own egg-father for a pet. I'd never gotten as much as a clown fish, and those were notoriously simple to keep.

I swam toward the market; my mate and I had heard the gatherers had found a large quantity of coconuts floating over the reef. No doubt a storm had blown them out of trees, which was a stroke of luck for our community. All seafolk loved coconut flesh; if I didn't hurry, I wouldn't be able to snap up one for my family's next meal.

I swam through the clear waters and the warm yellow sunbeams that reached below the surface to touch the white sands of the seafloor. It was so beautiful, so unlike the reef where I'd hatched. The sea there often had sediment in it from the rivers flowing off the land and the resulting cloudiness was ugly and tasted terrible as it flowed past your gills. I was grateful I'd found this reef, which was the native reef of my mate. When she'd chosen me to spread my milt over her eggs, I had achieved every male's dream: a beautiful reef home with a mate and eggs to hatch. This had become my new home.

It was easy to see where the coconuts were being kept. The crowd around that market stall and was thick and boisterous as merfolk shoved each other aside with arms and tails. Everyone wanted immediate access to the coconut vendor. As I approached, I saw I was too late. Tails flashed dark purple with disappointment rather than the bright green of excitement.

I hesitated, but there was no need to get closer. I'd just have to be faster next time I heard there were coconuts available.

I turned around and went back to the pet store, my own tail flashing disappointment. Upon reaching the pet shop, though, I did not see my hatchling. Or my mate. But then I spied my hatchling's pink-and-yellow scales inside the shop. My mate was with him. Her tail was a dull blue, tinged with green. She was in a good mood. I couldn't see why she would be, but apparently I was the only one in the family who found sea monkeys more irritating than anything else.

I swam into the shop. My mate and hatchling were observing a small bipedal creature standing in some sand. It had strange brown extensions on its head like dead seagrass. Its hide was almost the color of the sand tinged with pink like a youngster. It moved its mouth as if gulping air like a tadpole changing into a frog. I thought I heard some odd screeching sounds coming from the air bubble; perhaps it was singing like a whale or echolocating like a dolphin.

The sign on the tank read *Enter the world of the amazing Sea Monkeys! Own your own bubble of happiness.* In smaller characters it said *So eager to please. So easy to train!*

I must have read that out loud, because the hatchling said, "Train? What could I train it to do? Do you think it would come to its name or arrange the things in its bubble the way I want?"

"I doubt they're that trainable," I said.

"Oh, they're quite clever," said a new voice. I half-spun around to see an elderly male swimming up to us lazily. Probably the owner. "It can take them a while to understand at first, but realize, you must communicate through the barrier of water and air. It may not understand you are making deliberate gestures or sounds at first. But once it realizes you are trying to communicate directly with it, the training can proceed quickly."

"It won't live that long," I said. "Everyone I know who has gotten one has seen it die within days."

"I keep them healthy here in the shop," said the shopkeep. "They're a little trickier than other animals because their air must be refreshed daily and their water can have no salt in it. But in terms of food, they can eat almost anything from algae to fish."

"So air and water are the main things," said my mate. She looked contemplative and her gill slits waved gently and calmly. She was seriously considering this!

"We don't need the hassle or the expense," I said. "No hatchling is going to have the discipline to take care of a pet. I'll be the one who ends up doing everything for it. And if I do a good job keeping it alive, it could live for...?" I glanced at the shopkeep.

"Oh, they can live for years," he said. "I've heard that in their natural environment, they can live for decades."

"So it dies quickly due to bad air or bad water, or it could live longer than any of us."

The shopkeep just cocked his head in amusement. His tailfins flashed slightly orange. He knew he almost had us, considering the hatchling wanted it and my mate seemed agreeable.

"Perhaps we should just leave them in their natural environment," I said. "I have no wish to care of this thing for decades. By then even my hatchling's hatchlings will have surrendered their souls to the Sea Mother."

"But I want it!"

"It seems harmless enough," said my mate.

I tried a different tack. "At least with a fish, you can interact with it. Take it for a swim around the reef. This has to stay in the bubble."

"Ah, but we have new bubbles now, not like the old ones," said the shopkeep. "You can put your hand in through the barrier, as long as you do it from this side here," he pointed at the side of the bubble nearest to me. "See the slight purple glow? That will keep the bubble from collapsing when you put your hand through. Try it."

The hatchling eagerly shoved his hand through the barrier. The sea monkey immediately ran away. More mouth movements and the screeching sounds became slightly louder.

"How big will it get?" asked my mate. The sea monkey was easily the size of a fresh hatchling.

"Well, a bit bigger," said the shopkeep. "We try to trap youngsters, not full-grown adults. They're more trainable. You'll have to invest in larger bubbles every so often until it stops growing. We have special rates for those, as well as kits to refresh the air and water, and compact food packets, for those who've bought their sea monkey from us. But ultimately, it will grow to about half your size."

"We don't have that kind of room," I protested. "This will get *bigger*?" Honestly, our space on the reef was a bit tight for the three of us already. Three of us *and* an air bubble *and* the creature's supplies, *and* it would continue to grow?

"We can make do," said my mate.

The hatchling withdrew his hand. "It doesn't like me."

"Not yet," said the shopkeeper. "It was just captured yesterday. It hasn't had a chance to really get to know our ways under the sea yet. But soon you'll be able to play with it."

"Play?" asked the hatchling.

"Yes. Watch." The owner turned to another bubble. This one held a smaller sea monkey with long yellow grass growing from its head. It was easily more hatchling-sized. The owner picked up a small pebble, put his hand through the purple membrane on the side of the bubble, and tossed the pebble toward the sea monkey. It backed up at first, but then ran forward, picked up the pebble, and threw it back through the barrier.

The owner grabbed a small bit of blue-green algae and put his hand back inside the bubble. The sea monkey grabbed the algae eagerly and stuffed it in its mouth.

"They can eat quite a bit, especially once they figure out that you're feeding them. I don't think what we feed them resembles what they eat on land, but it's close enough for them to understand what's food and what isn't after a few tries."

"What do they eat besides algae?" asked my mate. She had leaned forward to study the smaller sea monkey.

"You can get some compressed pellets from us," said the seller. "Be sure to keep the pellets dry, though, because as soon as they get wet, they fall apart. Otherwise, pretty much anything we eat: algae, fish, molluscs. They're omnivores, just like us. Keep them away from pufferfish flesh and don't get salt in their water. That's about it."

Another merfamily swam into the shop.

"I'll just tend to these customers while you discuss the matter," said the seller. He swam leisurely toward the other family, who had bypassed the sea monkeys to look at the clown fish. Much more practical.

"I don't care what he says, they're still too delicate to keep. A clown fish, or even a skate, would be easier, and you could take it for daily swims out on the reef."

"Everyone has a clown fish," said the hatchling. His tail flashed the dark colors of disappointment. "I want something different. Something that's just mine. Not even Seawave's hatchling has a sea monkey."

So that was the real reason he needed an exotic pet. Seawave was an unbearably vain merman who was always going on about how his space on the reef was the best, how his mate was the most talented and laid the most eggs, and how perfect every single one of his hatchlings was. Everything in Seawave's life was perfect. Even the green stripes on his dorsal fins were exquisitely straight and brightly colored, unlike the rather muddy half-stripes of my mate and hatchling. I didn't even have stripes on my dorsal fins; merfolk hatched near the freshwater never did.

The mention of Seawave made my mate's face harden. She had endured taunting from his mate Moonlight on many occasions. Moonlight, in some ways, was even more unendurable than Seawave. She was not only perfect, she had chosen the perfect mate. No other merwoman on the reef could make such a claim. At least, not in Moonlight's presence.

"We can keep it alive," said my mate with an air of determination. She looked down at our hatchling, who was about to shiver his scales off in his excitement.

"The first one," he said. "The bigger one."

"No," I said. I couldn't believe I was giving up so easily. I suppose the mention of Seawave's name had affected me, too. "If you're going to get one, get the smaller one. It'll be younger and easier to train. It also knows one trick already."

"No," said the hatchling. "The bigger one."

"Talk to the seller," I said. "See what he suggests." Surely, he would agree that a smaller, more pliable sea monkey would be best.

My mate swam off, the hatchling right behind her. I glanced back at the original sea monkey. It sat in the far side of its bubble, on its pink sand beach, and glared at me. I swear, if the thing were intelligent, that look would mean it was plotting my death. Good thing they were too simple to have complex plans, let alone execute them.

I stuck my hand through the membrane and poked at the thing. It stood and backed up against the far side of the bubble. More mouth movements and sounds poured out of it. I reached for it.

Suddenly, the thing rushed forward, grabbed the finger I had extended toward it and bit down. I yelped, more in surprise than in pain and drew my hand back. I studied it a few moments, but I couldn't see any damage. The thing was really too small to hurt me. But the thought of it being aggressive and violent disturbed me. What if it bit my hatchling? The teeth that were too small to damage me could rip at his tender finger webs or fins. That wouldn't do.

The sea monkey and I stared at each other across the barrier. It made more noises and shook its hands in my direction. A cold hatred settled on me. I knew what I had to do.

I reached back in slowly. The sea monkey backed up, but the bubble was too small for it to get away from me. I grabbed at it and pushed its head back until I felt something snap in a most satisfactory way. The thing went limp.

I dropped it onto its pink sand and withdrew my hand. Let the thing try biting anything ever again! I went back over to the smaller sea monkey, which had witnessed the entire thing. The thing made noises and water came out of its eyes and ran down its face.

The seller swam back over with my mate and hatchling in tow. He glanced at the small sea monkey briefly. "Sometimes they do that," he volunteered. "Leak water from their eyes, I mean. It means they're upset. Give it a few days to settle in and it will be fine."

"But what upset it?" asked the hatchling.

"The other one," I said quickly. "It was throwing itself into the barrier, like it wanted to get out of its bubble."

"But it would drown!" said the hatchling.

"It doesn't know that," I said.

The seller glanced over. "Oh," he said curtly. "I see it's injured itself. Well, they do that sometimes. Most adapt to captivity over time, but some never do. Excuse me. I need to take care of this before other customers see it."

He swam over to the other bubble. My mate swam up beside me. "He convinced our hatchling to take the smaller one. Easier to keep."

"Especially since we're the ones who'll end up taking care of it," I said gruffly. "For years, assuming we can keep it alive for longer than a week."

She wrapped her tailfin around mine. "It will be fine," she said. "He explained how to change the air and water, and the pellets aren't very expensive. We can feed it scraps from our meals at first, to see what it likes best."

I knew when I was beat. "Sure," I said. "Why not? After all, if our hatchling can show up Seawave's hatchling, we can be duly proud."

"Absolutely." Her dorsal fin flashed between orange and yellow; she found the whole thing humorous.

"I can't wait to teach it more tricks!" our hatchling said. His tail could hardly get any brighter pink. That excitement would wear off after a few days of the reality of owning a pet. "I want to call it Sandflea."

"What a terrible name!" my mate exclaimed. "What about Sandripple? Or Coral Chimes?"

"No, no," said the hatchling. "It's small but moves quickly, like a sandflea."

The seller returned with the thing's bubble and supplies. "We can settle the purchase once I get it into its new environment," he said. His eyes were narrow with pleasure, like any seller who had just made money from a customer. "Then you can take it home and start with the feeding, playing, and training."

"Yeah," I said without enthusiasm. It took all my effort to keep my disappointment from showing on my tailfin. "We can get right on that."

My mate and hatchling swam toward the front of the store. I glanced back at the other bubble, but the seller had already removed the small body. *Good riddance.*

Sea monkeys. What a terrible pet!

At least the sea monkey would be easy to dispose of. If it became too annoying, I could take care of the matter. The thought comforted me as I watched my mate arrange for payment. My hatchling clutched the bubble against his chest while the sea monkey inside turned red from making mouth noises. It continued to leak water out of its eyes.

So impractical. So ugly. So expensive. Damn sea monkeys.

About the Author

Marella Sands is a native St. Louisan whose historical novels, *Sky Knife* and *Serpent and Storm*, were set in 5th century Central America. In 2021, her play "Kick in the Pants" was produced by First Run Theatre. Her play "Just a Coffee" will be produced by First Run Theatre in February 2025. Marella is currently working on two series: *Tales from the Angels' Share*, dark fantasy novellas starring a bartender who discovers her boss is something supernatural, and *Escaping Normal*, a non-fiction series on the paranormal. If you have a paranormal encounter you're willing to share, go to her website (marellasands.com) and click on "My Paranormal Story."

Marella and her husband travel whenever they can. Marella has visited many of the filming locations for the *Lord of the Rings* films in New Zealand. She had stood in the ruins of a city built by Alexander the Great, flown in a hot air balloon over the Bohemian countryside, and has actually been rained on in Death Valley. Still on her bucket list: Easter Island, the Namib Desert, and Shark Bay, Australia.

Marella never had sea monkeys as pets, despite seeing oodles of ads in comic books tempting children to do so.

True Skin

by

Cathryn H. Uber

True Skin

*M*other used to take me to see the mermaids.

She would be so sick and her belly would be so round. She would stay in bed, wrapped in blankets, not seeing anyone. I was always so tired when she got sick like that. I had to do everything for her. Not even the maids were allowed up to her room when she was very ill, Father wouldn't allow it. Mother always promised that as soon as she could, we would go see the mermaids. Finally, she would moan and writhe and send me to sit at the top of the stairs.

There is a groove where the floorboards meet at the top of the stairs. Almost imperceptible, but I could feel it. I would push on it when she grew loud, my hand hiding under my skirts, behind my knee, to find the spot.

Mother would come out eventually, in the early hours of the morning, and quietly bid me follow her. She leaned heavily on the wall, going down the steps. She always carried a small bundle after she had been ill.

More comfortable on the moonlit cobblestones in the salt-kissed air, we would walk out to the wharf, then follow the coast road out of town until it turned inland. Over the headland there was a small path—

"Made by the mermaids, to find their way home," she would smile, pale, brushing the wind-swept hair from my face. Like the tide, my silky brown hair had its own unpredictability. Her hair was forever smooth, shining as though wet, even in humid summer.

Once I asked why mermaids would need a path to come home. Her smile faded. "We all need a way home, even if we can't take it yet."

We trudged through the sandy dunes until we came to a small pier hidden in a cove. The dark predawn water lapped at the edges. The last stars reflected in the puddles on the wooden boards. Mother was no longer ill, here.

She would pull off her shoes, sit down with her skirts pulled up to her knees, and slowly put her feet in the water, relaxing as the chill of it washed her skin. She would breathe deeply, submerging a hand and washing her face before patting the pier next to her, inviting me down beside her.

We would sit there—me, and Mother, and the bundle—until all the stars had faded and the sky ahead of us had lightened. Then Mother would give a small giggle and pull me close.

I always felt them before I saw them, their fingers caressing my bare ankles, our shoes behind us on the worn wood. They would pull themselves up my legs, until three or four beautiful, scaly faces surrounded me, their thick twists of kelp and hair pulled back to reveal their wide eyes and wider mouths. They were so beautiful, so alien, and I was so drawn to them, but Mother would catch my shoulder and tsk: "She's still one of mine."

The mermaids always drew back, and I felt the cool, salty air upon my face again, though their long thin fingers still encircled my ankles.

Mother would bring the open bundle to her face and breathe in deeply, kissing inside the folds of cloth. When I was very young, she would send me back to the shore at this point, but when I could be trusted to keep this secret, she allowed me to stay. I never counted how many times we went to that pier with a bundle; sometimes we went without a bundle, but the mermaids didn't come those days. It was as if they knew which mornings Mother needed them.

"At dawn, mermaids come for secrets," Mother said in the beginning, as I wondered how many secrets she had given.

Mother would unwrap her bundle and reveal a beautiful seal pup sleeping in her arms. She would kiss the pup, holding it close, breathing deeply. Handing it gently to a mermaid, she would release it, and the scaled arms would pull the little one close, looking at the pup both with awe and with hunger. Another mermaid would rise from the water to wipe the salted tears from my mother's face.

"Take this one to join her sisters," Mother always said, and the mermaids would take the secret to the dark waves.

Then dawn would break, and as we walked home the fog would gather around us.

I asked once why Father did not come with us to see the mermaids when he was home between his long voyages. Mother's silence stretched for a long time.

"Or does he not know about the mermaids, Mother?"

"He knows about the mermaids, my child. He knows about many things under the ocean."

"Then why does he not come, Mother?"

After a long while, in a low voice, she said: "Do not speak to your father about the mermaids, dear. It will only anger him."

I did not mention the mermaids to Father. He was angry enough with his ships and voyages.

Once, Mother did not take me to see the mermaids after she was ill. She still grew round and writhed as usual, sending me out to perch at the top of the stairs. When she quieted, I waited for her to come out, so we could go see the mermaids. As time stretched on, and the sky lightened through the small window on the landing, she still did not come. Finally, just before I could feel the sun breaking across the horizon, the door behind me creaked open. I turned, expecting to hurry, scratching my leg on the grooved floorboard. She stood in the doorway, beckoning me to come.

"Mother?" I whispered. "Must we hurry?"

"No, child, not this time." She held something in her arms. Coming closer, I saw a little upturned face sleeping in the blankets. I looked up at Mother, confused. "He is your brother. Come and meet him."

We did not go to the mermaids that month, nor at the next full moon. Mother did not recover as quickly as usual. The maids were allowed up to attend to their normal duties, and Mother, full of joy, was so proud of her growing bundle. I missed the mermaids, but Mother was alight in a way I had never seen before.

Then Father returned.

I met him at the front door as I was expected to. He nodded to me as he usually did, handing me his bag. Looking around he sternly asked, "Where is she?"

The maids in the kitchen doorway curtsied, looking up the narrow stairs.

"Why isn't she here to greet me?" he asked tightly.

They wouldn't meet his eyes, and he didn't look at me.

His foot was heavy on the stairs. There was a tight feeling in my stomach.

I followed him up. His bag was always to be put on the chair by the window, and I wondered where I should put it since Mother had taken to sitting there with the baby.

The door slammed as I was still trying to climb the stairs with his heavy canvas bag. At the top of the stairs, I stopped, then turned and sat down. The groove was sharper now, with the heavy weight of the large sack on my lap.

"Get rid of it," I heard low through the door.

"He is yours," Mother said. "They are all yours."

"I'm not even sure the first one is mine," he growled. "But I've claimed her, so I'll take her and keep her—"

Mama wailed, a keening sound like the wind through the sails on a dark morning, the fog too thick to see the railing from the mast.

He said other things too, as I sat in the dark at the top of the stairs. Something heavy settled low in my stomach. No one ever came to fetch me. The sun slowly set behind the hills as I rubbed the sharp groove.

When the sky was very dark, the door creaked open behind me.

I turned, the wood scratching my leg again. I winced.

Mother stood in the doorway, sad, pale, a candle in her hand. Her nightgown hung on her hunched shoulders. She held a bundle on her hip. She slowly closed the door behind her.

"Are you going to see the mermaids, Mother?" I whispered.

She put the candle on the windowsill, then lifted the heavy bag from my lap, putting it down in front of the door as quietly as possible, wincing, but it did not creak. She relaxed, then offered her hand. I stood, reaching for her. She gave a small gasp.

At the top of the stairs was a little blood.

"I scratched my leg on the wood, Mother," I whispered. "It is nothing."

She made me turn around and lift my skirt so she could check. I twisted to look, too. The scratch had a few drops of blood, but then I saw a smear of blood higher up my leg. Mother seemed to sag.

I took a corner of my petticoat and scrubbed the spot at the top of the stairs, then the board moved and creaked. I paused; afraid I had woken Father. I looked to Mother.

She had frozen at the sound.

Then she seemed to see something. Looking down, I saw it too. The floorboard had moved.

She picked up the candle from the windowsill and crouched down beside me, the bundle wrapped with one arm.

"Gently," she said as quietly as possible.

I carefully lifted the board and moved it to the side, lowering it gingerly back to the floor. It didn't creak, and we both relaxed just a little.

She leaned the candle closer. It was still dark.

I reached in and touched something soft. It was heavy. With both hands, I maneuvered it out and lifted it up. The candlelight showed the hole was now empty.

We stood. Turning it over in my hands, it unraveled. Something small fell to the floor. Large and spotted with holes, I held up a large seal skin.

"Why—" I looked to my mother. She looked upon the seal skin as if it were a beautiful friend being returned to her. Her hands full with the candle and the bundle, she stepped closer, drawn to the dark velvet still remaining. She was mesmerized.

Through the door behind her, there was a snore.

We tensed again.

Then Mother moved quickly. Motioning with the candle, she had me gather up the seal skin and the small thing on the floor and hurry down the stairs. The pelt was still soft in my arms, though clearly it had been hidden for years. Outside it was darker than usual, but she still hurried us faster. She wasn't fully well, and we carried more than usual, the fur blocking my view of the cobblestones. She blew out the candle and tossed it away when we reached the dunes, the stars fading.

At the pier, she splashed the water with her empty hand, then rushed to remove her shoes, hurrying against the light.

"Unroll it, my daughter," Mother said, splashing the water again with her bare foot. "Hurry."

I unrolled the large skin on the pier behind her.

The mermaids were there when I turned around. She unwrapped the blankets from around the baby. The mermaids reached for him, their teeth shining in the lightening sky. Mother snatched him back. "This one is *mine*," she said with venom.

A mermaid on the side seemed to roll away into the water with disgust, making a small splash, the reflected pre-dawn light hiding the depths below. Another mermaid took him gently and sank beneath the waves.

Mother turned and saw the skin, a rare smile spreading across her face. She lifted the pelt, wrapped herself in it, seeming to glow with joy. She pulled me to her, embracing me tightly.

"Oh, we can go home. We can *go*," she said. She relaxed her hold on me, looking around the pier. "Where is the other one?"

I found it on the pier behind us. Carefully I unwrapped the canvas and revealed a piece of whalebone. Mother's face grew white, and she stiffened.

The whalebone had pictures on it. I peered closely. Waves were carved between a man and woman holding hands. I turned it over, feeling more carvings, and the line of light along the horizon brightened.

I looked to Mother, questioning.

"I was always interested in beautiful things. He carved many things on that, to pull me closer, then keep me. Be careful how they lure you." She pulled me close again, smoothing my windswept hair. "Do not be trapped by pretty toys."

She held me. I felt the sunlight break across the sky, warming my skin. She took my chin and lifted my face. "I cannot take you with me, my pup, my girl, not while your father has your skin. But one day, you may find it, and the mermaids will bring you home to me."

She wiped the tears from her face, sprinkling them in the water. "When it is hard, remember: seven tears will call a seal man to your side."

The mermaids parted and a man came up out of the water between them, as if climbing stairs. Water dripped from him as he stood in front of Mother, offering his hand. He was tall, like Father, but he stood stronger, younger, reaching out to Mother as if he would gather all of her into him, as though he could find no fault with her. She smiled more widely than I had ever seen. The gray hair at her temple seemed to darken, her face seemed to smooth. She released me, took his hand and stepped into the water after him, sinking out of sight. The mermaids came back together against the edge of the wooden boards, a few reaching up to caress my feet. From above, I could see their long tails stretched down into the empty dark.

Then they, too, sank into the water.

I stood on the pier long after the sun had risen.

About the Author

A jack of all trades and a master of some, Cathryn H. Uber is a writer, teacher, and editor who prefers to run away to the mountains with manuscripts whenever possible. Cathryn earned a Masters in Humanities focusing on the Great Books and what literature reveals about the cultures that produce it from American Military University, an MBA focused on digital marketing also from American Military University, and a Masters in Creative Writing with an emphasis in Publishing from Western Colorado University (not concurrently) after earning her Associates in General Studies and Bachelors in Creative Writing from Brigham Young University. Her Bachelors culminated in a staged reading of her play, which she wants to put on stage again but she's a little too busy for nightly rehearsals.

Cathryn has written "True Skin," published by Knight Writing Press, *Diner Talk*, produced as a staged reading in 2016, and many others. She has edited a number of books and anthologies, including the *Once Upon A Future Time* series, published by The Brothers Uber.

Cathryn and her husband Logan pile the husky-shepherd lap dog, the toddler princess, the artist stepdaughter, and the gamer stepson into the van every summer as they see how many National Parks they can visit before school starts again. She is constantly writing something: lesson plans, analysis, essays, fiction, or creative nonfiction, usually in an attempt to process the incredible swath of stars sprawled across midnight skies far from advancing city lights. Find her work at brothersuber.com.

The Skeletal Leaf

by

Sam Knight

The Skeletal Leaf

*F*arrah Ceilpe, winter business coat draped over her legs and half covering the briefcase in her lap, nudged the electric wheelchair's joystick toward the mahogany bookshelf. She leaned forward for a closer look at the perfectly preserved, mounted and framed specimen. It looked like a large, black, broad leaf with starkly contrasted and delicate, white venation that eerily looked like finger bones.

"The staff call that the Skeletal Leaf," a deep voice said. "It's probably obvious why."

Farrah turned her wheelchair to find an elderly man entering the office, leaning heavily upon his cane with each step he took toward the desk at the back of the small room. Though hunched over, Director Caldwell still towered over Farrah's small, seated figure. She watched him make his way past shelves overflowing with books and maps and specimens. The back wall was reserved for the flag of the United States, the Department of State Seal, a plaque that stated Office of Oceanic Conservation, and a portrait of the president. The shuffling old man, large as he was, somehow looked small and colorless beneath those dominating images.

"That is the rare species you claimed was wiped out by the invasive kelp forests?" Farrah asked, keeping her coat in front of her like a protective shield.

"One of the many." The man thumped his cane on the floor emphatically. "I first learned of it years ago, before anyone else had even started thinking about conservation. I keep it there to remind me of my *real* purpose. No one else in modern memory has ever encountered such a specimen, and now they never will." The man glanced stiffly over his shoulder at her and chuckled.

"Oh! Don't tell me you are a doubter of its authenticity, too!" he said, shaking his gray head. "I know it is distinct and unique, unlike any other plant ever found, but I expected more from the great Farrah Ceilpe who graduated at the top of her class, had a meteoric rise through the ranks, and comes so highly recommended as to—nearly miraculously—become my replacement. No easy feat, that." He mumbled the last words, as though giving the compliment was painful.

"You know," he continued, "Ceilpe means *kelp* in Gaelic. It's almost like you were destined for this kind of work."

"Scottish Gaelic, actually." Farrah moved her wheelchair in front of the desk as the man shuffled into place behind it and dropped into his leather chair, as if to make sure she knew it was still his. "And I guess you could say I was called to this kind of work. I've always had a strong affinity for the oceans. The studies and research came naturally to me, and conservation, well, sometimes that part seems to hit a little close to home, doesn't it? I felt this is where I need to be."

She met the old man's gaze. "And I am not a *doubter*. Shakespeare's quote would have been just as accurate to say 'in the sea as in Heaven and Earth,' but I am sure your experience has already taught you that as well, Mr. Caldwell."

"Indeed, it has." Caldwell adjusted his glasses and squinted at her. "Tell me, young lady, have we met before?"

"I am surprised and flattered to think you might recognize me aside from my file. We've barely passed in the crowd despite running in the same circles. I have been fortunate enough to have attended a few of your lectures over the years. Your thoughts on practicing conservation by destroying so many of the individual kelp forests were, and still are, controversial, to say the least."

Caldwell, glasses perched on the end of his nose as he looked at his phone, grunted in response. "To say the very least. But if you want to make an omelet…"

After a moment of silence, he looked from his phone and back to Farrah. When she didn't respond, he seemed to finally take notice of a small box on his desk.

"That's for you," Farrah said. "I know you feel you're being forced out of this position."

"Forced out," he agreed with another mumble. "Age discrimination is what it is. One or two health problems and mistakes…" His voice trailed off.

"Your *mistake* ordered millions of gallons of herbicide to be dumped on what may have been the last of the great kelp forests. It is an ecological disaster. Not to mention it directly countered the wishes of your opposition."

Farrah thought she saw him smile faintly at that. He didn't respond to her comment, though. Instead, with aged, tremoring hands, Caldwell opened the box and looked inside.

"It works," she said. "Though it takes a battery, not gas, obviously."

He lifted out the tiny, antique replica Johnson Sea Horse outboard motor, his shaky fingers somehow switching on the tiny button on the base of the stand. The high-pitched whine of the spinning propeller sounded correct, even in miniature.

Caldwell glanced from the replica in his hand to the identical motor on the back of the small boat in the photograph on his desk. A much younger version of himself, grinning broadly, stood in front of the boat, arm around the waist of a beautiful young woman. Though the photograph was black and white, he could still see her fiery red hair, and he fell back seventy years, into the memory of a newlywed.

The little boat, bobbing in the gentle moonlit waves, began drifting away from the dock.

"Come on, Cob, hurry!" Wendy, inside the boat, sat her lantern down and flapped her arms desperately. "I'm going to end up lost at sea! Jump!"

With a leap from the dock, Jimmy Caldwell soared through the air and cleared the Johnson Sea Horse motor on the back of the boat, landing hard on the back bench, the jolt knocking over the lantern. For a moment, he, the boat, and Wendy all teetered on the edge of going over. Wendy shrieked, holding tight to the sides, her voice breaking into laughter as Jimmy finally caught his balance and pretended to be on a high wire.

"I thought you weren't going to call me Cob anymore after we got married," he said, one leg raised and arms still wheeling in a circle.

"And I thought—" She gasped as he purposely fell into a sitting position on the bench, sending out waves and shaking the boat again. "And I thought I told you I'd stop calling you Cob when you stopped being *corny.*"

"Okay, *Missus Cob.*"

"At least I'm a missus *somebody.*"

Something in Wendy's voice caught Jimmy's attention as he tugged the rope to start the motor. The motor sputtered and purred to life, spitting out blue smoke that settled and drifted across the calm waves like a miniature fog.

"What does that mean?" he called to her over the noise.

"What do you think it means?" She raised an eyebrow and looked at him slyly.

"That you're an Able Grable who would have married anyone who came along and asked?" He gunned the motor, making her grab hold again.

"Don't be a crumb! Where are you taking me?"

"Do you know what today is?"

"Saturday?"

"We," Jimmy said adjusting the trim as the boat picked up speed, "have been married for exactly six months to the day!" Whooping, he pushed the tiller and changed direction sharply, forcing Wendy to grab for the sides again to keep from falling out. The whites of her eyes and teeth shone in the orange glow of the lantern as she grinned madly and whooped with him.

They didn't talk for fifteen minutes, as the wind stole any words, whipping them away before they could be heard. Jimmy finally aimed the boat toward a quiet bay and dropped speed as they approached buoys and a rope that cordoned off the entire beach. He killed the motor and let the boat continue to drift forward in the suddenly quiet night.

"Where are we?" Wendy asked.

"A private place." Jimmy stood and stepped to reach over her, down into the water. He caught hold of the heavy rope. "Duck," he told her as he lifted it out of the water and held it up so the small boat could pass under.

"Hey!" Wendy giggled as the rope went over her head and dripped water on her dress. "You're getting me all wet."

"You're about to get a lot wetter," Jimmy said, dropping the rope behind the boat. "We are going to swim to that beach, and I am going to make love to you in the moonlight. Our own little paradise, just you and me, all alone, on our half-anniversary." He leaned close and looked into her eyes. "I love you."

"I love you, too, Jimmy." She gave him a quick kiss. "But we won't *really* be alone."

"We will. I asked around. This place is abandoned, has been for years. Some old coot made it some kind of preserve when he died."

"That's not what I mean." Wendy's voice dropped as low as the water gently lapping the side of the boat. "I'm pregnant."

Jimmy froze, his eyes moving back and forth between hers. "No foolin'?"

"No foolin', Mr. Caldwell. You're gonna be a daddy."

Jimmy stood tall in the boat, glowing in the warm lantern and cool moonlight, threw back his head and whooped. "You hear that, world? I'm gonna be a daddy!"

He quickly stripped off his shirt and pants and dove into the black water. "Come on in, the water's fine!"

Wendy fussed with her dress for a moment and then, modestly covering herself, set the lantern up on the bow of the boat before following her husband into the inky waters. Her giggles carried through the night as she swam toward Jimmy and caught his hand. He pulled her close and they kissed, gently bobbing in the waves.

When they broke apart, Wendy gasped and gripped him tightly. "What is that?"

"Oh, I think you know!"

"Stop it. I mean in the water. Something is…"

"Yeah. It's just seaweed. I think there's a ton of it here because it's roped off and no boats ever come in."

"It's slimy. I don't like it, Jimmy."

"Come on. Let swim to the beach." He tugged at her hand and pulled her along.

Flinching repeatedly, as though many things brushed her skin under the water, Wendy kicked her feet and went along with him.

"It's getting worse," Wendy gasped between strokes. "It's everywhere now. I feel like it's going to grab me and pull me under."

"Don't be silly. It's just water weeds. We're halfway there. It'll be worth it. You'll see."

"Jimmy! I feel like I can't swim through it!"

He stopped pulling and moved back closer to Wendy. "Hey. It's okay. I've got you."

"I'm tangled up in it!" She jerked her arm, the movement putting her face under water.

Jimmy caught her, kicking his own legs harder to keep her up. He found her arm, found the weeds tangled around it, and yanked.

The plant broke free but remained wrapped around her arm.

"I want to go back to the boat." Wendy's voice was panicky and her eyes, wide in the moonlight, desperately searched his face for agreement.

"Okay, okay. Come on. Let's go back. We can take the boat to shore instead."

The light from the small lantern on the bow of the boat seemed miles away in the night. Struggling against the panic and the heavy drag created by the seaweed strand they couldn't get unwrapped from her arm, Wendy was exhausted by the time they reached the boat. She couldn't pull herself in even with Jimmy pushing from behind.

"Just hold on to the side, okay?" he told her. "I'm going to climb in, and then I'll pull you up. All you have to do is hold on to the side and rest a minute, okay?"

Wendy nodded and gasped for air, panting from the exertion. The boat listed hard as Jimmy pulled himself in, causing Wendy's head to dunk below water again, and she came up sputtering. Then Jimmy had her, lifting her, pulling her out of the water and into the refuge of the little boat.

They sat naked, exhausted, eyes not looking at anything out in the night, as Wendy held tightly to him.

"I think I've had enough excitement for one night," she said.

"Okay." He squeezed her close. "Okay."

"Can you get this off? It's hurting."

Jimmy sat up and looked at the seaweed still pulling on Wendy's arm like a shackle tethering her to the water. He tugged at it until she cried out in pain.

"I think we need to cut it off," she said. "It's too strong."

"It's just knotted somehow. Here, let's get some slack." Jimmy grabbed the vine-like stalk hanging over the side and pulled. "It's heavy."

"I *know*."

Whenever he let go, it quickly pulled back down, heavy with weight on the far end. Bringing more of the weed into the boat, its wet leaves shimmering in the lamplight, he tried to hold it from sliding back into the water with his foot while he worked to untie her wrist, but everything was too slimy.

Frustrated, he quickly began pulling the whole thing in, hand over hand, piling it into the bottom of the boat. At the end, he lifted a heavy, gelatinous lump, nearly the size of a watermelon, and brought it into the boat.

"Ugh! What is that?"

"I don't know. Some kind of egg sac." Jimmy grabbed the lantern and brought it in close to see. There was a form inside the bulbous mass, and it seemed to react to the light, spinning around inside. He lifted the stalk, raising the thing into the air, and held the lantern behind it to illuminate the shape inside.

Wendy gasped. "Jimmy. That looks like a baby!"

"With a tail…" he added.

"Get this off of me, Jimmy! Get it off!"

"Okay!" Jimmy dropped the thing back to the bottom of the boat and began digging under the bench seats and pulled out a duffle. It took only a moment to find the sheathed knife within.

"Hold still," he told her.

"It's not me, it's the boat," she protested, but her breath was shallow and quick as her bare body shivered in the lamplight.

Holding slimy leaves out of the way so he could see, he wedged the tip of the blade between her skin and the slippery vine. When the seaweed fell free from her wrist, Wendy sighed heavily and wrapped her arms around herself.

"Here. Get dry." Jimmy pulled a towel from the duffel and tossed it to Wendy.

"Can we go home? Please?"

"Yeah. I'm sorry this turned out miserable. It wasn't what I had planned." He lifted the egg sac up and held it in front of the lantern again, peering at the dark form moving inside.

"It's hideous," Wendy complained. "Throw it back. Get rid of it."

"I want to know what it is." Jimmy brought the tip of the knife to the sac and cut a long slice down the transparent side. A slimy substance, like raw egg white, viscously dripped out, followed by the small creature inside.

It landed in the bottom of the boat, flailing its fish-like tail and human-like arms. When it opened its mouth and took a breath, it wailed like a baby, Wendy screamed.

"What the holy—!" Jimmy was interrupted by an explosion of water on the side of the boat.

A slender, dark-skinned figure, eyes and teeth flashing in the lamplight, landed half-in, half-out of the boat. Its slick, wet skin glistened in the lamplight as it scrabbled for the tiny, squalling creature flopping about in the mess of seaweed between Jimmy and Wendy.

Wendy reacted first, jumping up and shrieking, kicking her bare feet at the monstrosity, trying to force it out of the boat. She connected solidly with it, but instead of kicking it out, she knocked herself over backward and out of the boat.

"Wendy!" Jimmy roared, a scream of primal rage and terror. The knife in his hand flashed out to stab at the creature crawling into his boat as it grabbed for the disgusting hatchling. Eyes locked, the creature and Jimmy were held frozen as a momentary eternity passed between them. And then both of their faces twisted. The creature's in rage and anguish; Jimmy's in revulsion and horror at the human features on such an inhuman creature.

The creature, clutching the slimy infant to its chest with one hand, swiped the other at Jimmy's face just as he slashed the knife at it again. The knife caught the creature at its thin wrist, severing its hand, which slapped against Jimmy's face and fell to the bottom of the boat. Screaming, the creature threw itself away from Jimmy, taking the hatchling with it as it fell back into the ocean.

"Jimmy!" Wendy's scream tore Jimmy's attention away from where the creature had vanished. "Jimmy! Help me!" Wendy floundered, trying to get back to the boat which was drifting away from her.

"I'm coming! Hold on!" Jimmy jumped to the end of the boat and yanked on the outboard motor's pull rope, firing up the engine just as he saw the wake plowing through the waves, heading for Wendy.

"No!" he cried. "No!" He gunned the motor and spun the boat toward her, but his speed was no match for the thing in the water.

Wendy saw it coming and slapped her hands against the water, trying to move out of the way. It hit her hard, the impact snapping her neck sideways and lifting her up out of the water, the creature carrying her yards before coming back down. Both disappeared under the waves and the empty night went silent except for the sound of the motor and Jimmy's screams.

Caldwell pressed the button that turned off the little electric motor. He looked up at Farrah. "Very thoughtful of you," he said, his voice cracking and stilted. "I haven't seen a motor like this in decades. It brings back memories of long, long ago."

For a moment, neither of them said anything.

"I'm sorry," Caldwell said, coming back into focus. He reached into his pocket and pulled out a handkerchief to wipe his nose. "It reminded me of my wife. She died a very long time ago. Tragic accident. A shark attack."

"That's not the way I remember it," Farrah said.

Caldwell looked up sharply. Farrah removed her jacket and briefcase from her lap, setting them on the ground, and, for the first time, Caldwell saw she had no feet resting on the footplates and she was missing her right hand.

Pressing the joystick, she spun her wheelchair and turned her back on him, steering back to the specimen mounted on the bookshelf. Raising her arm, she reached up and placed her remaining hand, with her long, thin fingers, upon the glass, covering the so-called Skeletal Leaf. It was a near perfect match.

"I did recognize you!" Caldwell hissed the words at her, his gray eyes flashing with anger as he heaved his body up out of the chair and slammed his palms on the desk. "You killed my wife and unborn child!"

Farrah didn't flinch. "You killed my child first. And then dozens more as you rampaged with your motorboat that night, tearing up everything with that propeller—"

"I was trying to find Wendy!"

"And since, you've killed thousands upon thousands of my people's children by intentionally poisoning and mowing down our nurseries." Hardly a whisper, her voice was cold and emotionless.

"It wasn't enough!" he snarled at her.

"You're right." Farrah turned and squared her shoulders at him. "It wasn't. Because despite your best efforts over the last sixty years of your *career*, my people still live. And now that *I* am in charge of your horrid office of *conservation*, the *mistakes* I am about to make will be much more effective against humans than you were against us."

"I'll kill you!" Caldwell lurched around the desk, grabbing for his cane, brandishing it as a weapon. After only two steps, he fell to the floor, shaking.

"That would be the neurotoxin I put on the toy motor," Farrah said, rolling closer and looking down into his wild eyes. "It comes from a very small fish that, like so many of the wonderful things in the ocean, is still unknown to your kind. It will conveniently make it appear you had a heart attack. Easily attributable to you being upset at the unexpected arrival of your replacement."

She reached over the desktop, picked up the tiny antique motor and turned it over in her hand, pushing the button and turning the tiny propeller on and off. "I thought it a fitting delivery mechanism. So ironic, don't you think?" She packed it back into the box and then pulled a wipe from her chair's side pocket. Her voice grew stronger as she carefully wiped off the box and then everywhere she could reach where the motor might have touched. "Fortunately, my kind is immune to the toxin, but I wouldn't want my new secretary to accidentally touch it, would I? At least not before we finish flooding your food and water supply with it."

Farrah nudged the wheelchair around the corner of the desk. She wiped the rest of the desk and then lifted the phone receiver from the office desk and dialed the operator. "This is Office of Oceanic Conservation Director Farrah Ceilpe requesting emergency assistance. Former Director James Caldwell has collapsed while in the process of vacating his office."

As she waited for the emergency response team, Farrah went back to look at the framed specimen and allowed herself the slightest smile as she ran over Cob's hand on the way. "If you don't mind," she said without looking down to Caldwell, "I think I'll keep this right here in the office. As a reminder of *my* real purpose."

About the Author

Sam Knight is the owner/publisher of Knight Writing Press and author of six children's books, four novels, and over 90 short stories, including three co-authored with Kevin J. Anderson. Though he has written in many cool worlds, such as Planet of the Apes, Wayward Pines, and Jeff Sturgeon's Last Cities of Earth, among his family, Sam will probably always be known for *Chunky Monkey Pupu*.

Once upon a time, Sam was known to quote books the way some people quote movies, but now he claims having a family has made him forgetful—as a survival adaptation.

The Maxy Mermaid

by

Angelique Fawns

The Maxy Mermaid

My grandfather, King Dragonfish, summoned me to his office in the Oceanus palace. Seashells and coral glittered on the walls behind his throne of whalebone. His long silvery beard couldn't hide his scowl.

"Mira, you're approaching your second decade. It is time you found yourself a decent merman and settled down. You cause me so much grief." He struck the ground with his trident.

"Why don't you stick that trident up—"

"Silence! You don't want to spend more time in the sea dungeon, do you?"

I pressed my lips together to bite back my next smart-ass remark, I'd been sent to the watery hell under the castle before. The sea dungeon was burgeoning with merfolk who'd somehow offended my mercurial grandfather. The conditions were horrendous. Overcrowding, rotten seafood, and crab infestations.

Short on coral tax? Sea dungeon.

Slack off during volunteer hours cleaning his bone collection? Sea dungeon.

Dare to challenge his image of the perfect cis merfamily? Offenders are lucky to get the sea dungeon.

Grandfather's two goons, Spike and Storm, moved toward me. They were burly, ugly guys, both with scarred faces and missing bits of fin.

I bowed and plastered a submissive smile on my face. "As you wish, Grandfather."

The goons paused.

"You are dismissed," King Dragonfish said with a final thump of his trident.

Swimming out of the office, I caught the eye of his secretary, Gabriella. Butterflies tickled my gut as I blew her a kiss. She still had bruises on her arm from Storm dragging her away from me last week. We'd been caught sharing cuddles behind the coral reef. We'd both ended up in the dungeon that day. I know Octavia, my uptight sister, snitched. Perfect Octavia with her perfect warrior merman, was more about her inheritance than sisterly love.

I'd confronted her yesterday. "Octa-venom, you know snitches get stitches, right?"

She'd just laughed. We looked so much alike with our long, dark hair and ebony skin. But somehow she'd ended up with the cruel edge of our father and I was more like our long-dead mother. When I confided to my grandmother about my crush on Fiona (only my best friend forever) at thirteen, she'd stood up to my grandfather. Then she'd died from a mysterious poisoning.

King Dragonfish was a cold one alright. He had replaced my gram with a nubile new bride within the week. And I didn't even have parents I could turn to. A run-in with a rabid squid left me orphaned a decade ago.

His secretary, Gabriella, grabbed my arm as I passed her. She fluttered those long lashes, gave me a quick smile, and subtly slid a laminated brochure into my hand. "Don't look at it here. It comes from the world above the waves."

My stomach flipped as I tucked the card into the cup of my top. I left the palace and swam to my favorite place to think. My secret cave was hidden behind spiky red sea whip plants. Taking out the brochure, I read the information, eyes widening.

Memorial Day Weekend! The Provincetown Lesbian Festival. Race Point Beach. Saturday, May 28th.

I could only dream about attending an event like this. Was Gabriella being a cruel tease, or giving me hope? That was this weekend! A deep longing clenched my heart. There was only one woman I had ever truly loved. I scratched at the green algae on the cave wall until two names carved into the stone were visible.

Mira + Fiona.

Cuddling with Gabriella had been a bit of fun, but Fiona was the real thing. This cave had been our sanctuary. Running my fingers over the names, I choked back a sob and floated to the sea floor. There were divots in the cave wall where Fiona had repeatedly practiced her gymnastics. Her tail was so strong it dug out little chunks as she flipped, her lower body twisting and turning like a dolphin.

My best friend and lover had been ferocious, athletic, and determined to escape from my grandfather's homophobic reign.

I lost myself in a memory from five years ago in this very cave.

"We can swim away and join the Oceanus circus. They take mermaids like us. Misfits," she said, kissing the newest scar on my cheek. "If you keep fighting the King's guards, you'll end up dead."

"What would I do in the circus? You can do amazing flips. I'm only good at two things; fighting and swimming fast." I stroked her sleek purple hair.

She pursed her rosebud lips. "At least we will be together."

"You know that if you leave Oceanus, you can never come back." My guts churned at the idea. I thought of myself as a rebel, but Fiona was next level.

The spark in Fiona's eyes flared. "I'm so tired of sneaking around. And I can't handle the dungeon."

I didn't believe she'd actually leave. But then one day she was gone.

All she'd left was a note. *If you ever change your mind, come find me at the circus!*

Three months later, when the Cirque du Merlay came to Oceanus, I bought a ticket. Fiona wasn't part of the troupe. I'd lost her with no idea of where she was.

Shuddering, I wiped away a tear and wrenched my mind back to the present.

This cave was all I had left of her. It wasn't enough. Rubbing my fingers over our names, I resolved to change my life. If I couldn't be true to Fiona, at least I could be true to myself. I plunged out of the cave, flapping my tail with strength and determination. No way I was marrying some old merman and having a bunch of guppies. Gabriella had given me some hope with that pamphlet. The Lesbian Festival would be a start.

One problem.

I needed legs if I was going to mingle with human honeys.

There was only one woman who I knew could help me. A witch as diabolical as my grandfather. My blood iced. Making deals with Endora sometimes turned ugly. But she was my only option.

A school of bluefish swam beside me, but I outpaced them easily. After an hour of hard swimming, I found the hidden lair. Right where the whispers and rumors described it. An old monster skeleton that was covered in zombie worms.

Home of Endora, the sea witch. She was part octopus, part human. All evil.

Before I could lose my nerve, I dove into the main hall, skirting the writhing polyps, and stopped outside the main hall doorway.

"Come in, my darling. We don't lurk, do we? It's rude," Endora said.

She beckoned with her octopi tentacles, her wild, white hair waving around her head. I moved through the waterproof barrier and approached her throne. She plucked a live shrimp from the clam beside her, slurping enthusiastically.

"Maybe Mira would like some shrimp? She's always hungry," a familiar voice said from the corner.

Joy burbled up in my throat as my heart swelled with happiness. A mermaid with a purple mohawk was stirring a cauldron. Fiona. Looking every bit as gorgeous as I remembered. It had been five years since I saw her last. She hadn't aged a day.

My cheeks burned pink. "Fiona, I thought you joined the sea circus? You look—" I heard the tremor in my voice. My heart pounded double time.

Fiona shot me a dark look. "It didn't work out. In fact, it was pretty terrible. If you'd been brave enough to come with—" Fiona stabbed in my direction with her long spoon.

"What happened to you?"

"Turns out the circus had enough gymnasts," she said, her mouth a hard line. "They turned me away. You know your grandfather exiles those who dare to leave." She stirred the potion in the cauldron. "I had nowhere else to go but here."

I tried to give Fiona a hug, but Endora caught me with her tentacles.

"I'm not interested in your lovers' reunion. I'm assuming you are here for business?" the sea witch asked.

With shaking hands, I took out the brochure. "King Dragonfish is forcing me to marry, but—"

"Mermen don't float her boat." Fiona slapped the ground with her tail.

"And you want legs so you can go to this festival and find your true love?" Endora yawned.

"I'd like legs so I can live and love who I like." I raised an eyebrow.

Endora dismissed me with a wave. "Boring."

"Is revenge boring? How about I'm looking for revenge?" I asked.

"Better."

"Think how humiliated King Dragonfish will be if the whisper mill hears of me living on the land as a lesbian human? What if he can't control one little, rebellious granddaughter?"

"The homophobic old fart." Endora smiled.

"So, I can go?" I asked, slipping out of her tentacles. "Maybe Fiona can come with me?" I smiled her way, but my ex-lover avoided my gaze.

"Fiona must stay here. She made her own deal." Endora picked out a fat shrimp. "But you... Can you pay the price?"

Fiona moved away from the cauldron, her fins quivering. "She's got nothing. Endora, send her home."

I furrowed my brow. Was Fiona jealous, or warning me?

Endora got up from her chair, flapping a tentacle at me in dismissal. "If you have nothing to barter with—"

"My swimming ability! I'm the best swimmer in the kingdom." I swam in a tight circle, showing off my powerful fins.

Endora tickled her chin with her tentacles. "You will give me your swimming ability, and I will grant your wish for legs for twenty-four hours."

"Only twenty-four hours?"

"If you find your true love in twenty-four hours, the power of love will override my spell, and you can keep your legs," Endora said, yawning again.

"Thank you," I said, clapping my hands together.

"Don't thank her yet. There is always a caveat," Fiona said.

Endora spit out a shrimp tail. "If you don't find your 'true love' in twenty-four hours, you will return to Oceanus, and I will keep your remarkable swimming power."

"I'll be a mermaid who can't swim?" I widened my eyes.

"You will swim. But more like an old sea slug than a dolphin," Endora said.

"And?" Fiona asked.

Endora shot an irritated look at Fiona. "Who made you part of the negotiations?"

"Tell her," Fiona said.

Endora turned to me. "One more warning. If you get wet while on land, you will turn back into a mermaid. It will be up to you to find your way home."

I paused and looked at Fiona. There was a time I could read her every mood. But I couldn't tell if she even cared about me anymore. The light in her eyes was gone. That alone broke my heart. Fiona had broken my heart more than once. The way she fled to the circus, leaving only a note...

Fiona smacked the ground with her tail again. "If you lose your swimming ability, what will you have?"

All the old hurt flooded back. "I'm done with sneaking around, Fiona. If you cared about me, you wouldn't have left."

She lifted her chin. "And if you cared more about me, you would have joined the circus."

The same argument we'd had five years ago still made me hot and furious. "I'll take the deal."

Endora handed me a waterproof human watch. "You'll need this."

I strapped it on. Both hands pointed straight up to the XII. It was noon.

Fiona sucked her teeth. "Okay, this is how it works. You'll drink this potion." She siphoned some liquid out of the cauldron and into a cup. "You'll wake up with legs on a little island. A whale-watching tour boat from Provincetown stops there once a week. They let the tourists out onto the island for a few minutes to collect seashells. Slip onto the boat."

"Why don't you come with me?" I grabbed her in a hug after sipping my bitter drink.

Endora threw a shrimp tail at me. "She's happy here!"

I seriously doubted that my energetic friend was happy trapped here, so I cautiously touched her muscular arm. This time I would fight for her.

"You had your chance." Fiona pushed me away. "You have three hours before the tour boat arrives. It leaves at 3:00 p.m. I suggest you use that time to get used to your new legs. Hike up the mountain."

When I woke up on the white sand, the sun was warm on my skin. A light dress, as blue as the sky, lay beside me and I slipped it on. Wiggling brown toes, I smiled at my new long legs. My hair was tied up in a high ponytail with a green ribbon. The hilly island looked deserted, except for the chirping birds in the trees behind me.

The watch gave a beep. It was 12:10 p.m.

There were a few hours to wait, so I went for a hike up the big hill behind me, as per Fiona's advice. Mosquitos nibbled on my skin and the path was rough, but the view was worth it. Blue Atlantic water, white-capped waves, and the shadow of Cape Cod in the distance.

Looking down at the beach, I saw a boat had dropped anchor. Like tiny crabs, the tourists were packing up their towels. They were scuttling to get on a small boat that would take them back to the whale-watching ship.

"Hey! Wait for me!" It was useless. No one would hear me from here.

I checked my watch. 1:00 p.m. Fiona had said three hours!

Why did I trust her?

Running back down the trail, the plants and rocks conspired against me. Roots entwined around my ankles. Pebbles bruised my bare feet. Twice I fell to the ground, rolling like a beach ball. My lungs ached when I finally reached the beach, but the shuttle was already loaded and sailing.

"No! You can't go! Come back!"

The waves were too loud. The tourists were distracted.

Could I swim to the shuttle and catch it? I was just about to splash into the foamy surf when Endora's words echoed in my memory:

"If you get wet while on land, you will turn back into a mermaid."

There wouldn't be another boat for a week. The spell was for twenty-four hours.

The ship's horn blared as it sailed parallel to the island. Ignoring the burning in my calves, I ran along the shore, keeping a healthy distance from the surf. The whale-watching boat was going to pass very close to the peninsula's edge. My toe caught on driftwood, and I tripped headfirst into the sand. The pain from a twisted ankle bolted up my leg. The boat sailed around the edge of the island and vanished from sight. Tears streamed down my red-hot face.

Turns out the view hadn't been worth it.

My guts roiled.

Thump. Thump. Rump, rump, thump. A beat rang out over the beach.

I raised my head from the sand, spitting out the wet granules.

Thump. Rump, thump, rump, thump. The noise was coming from somewhere in the forest.

I hoisted myself up with a grunt. My ankle throbbed. Soaking it in cold salt water would probably help. But, once again, I could not get wet.

Several feet away, I saw brownish-orange seaweed clinging to some rocks and grabbed a handful. I wrapped my ankle in the slimy material, held together with the hair ribbon. Seaweed was used at home to treat all sorts of injuries. The redness and swelling immediately subsided, and the ribbon from my ponytail secured the bandage to my ankle.

Rump, rump. Thump, rump.

It sounded like music. A heavy dance beat. I limped into the woods and followed a path along a stream. The music got louder, and I could see a break in the trees. I was so focused on my destination; I didn't notice the man on the side of the path until he spoke.

"Took yourself for a pee, did you? There are potties at the party." He leered at me, fingering the fuzz on his upper lip, like he was trying to grow a mustache and failing.

What kind of folks lived in the world above the waves? I'd imagined them all perfect, like princes and princesses. But there were degenerates in the two-legged world just as there were back home. Grandfather's goons, Spike and Storm came to mind. This guy was just as gross. A teenage hoodlum.

"I need a boat," I said, giving him a quick once over. He was wearing cut-off jeans and a bandanna around his head.

"A pretty girl like you all alone in the woods? I know what you need." He slapped my bum and I started. Human flesh was far more sensitive than scales.

I took the seaweed bandage off my ankle. "Do that again."

"You liked it, did you?"

This time before he could make contact, I whipped the seaweed around his throat and pulled. The bandage had dried into a thin, strong rope with my ribbon as its core. The man's eyes bulged. He struggled, but I held tight. When he collapsed, I checked his pulse and it was still there. Faint but throbbing. This fellow was a reminder of what awaited me back home if I didn't successfully find true love. I'd end up in the clutches of goons with tails.

I walked toward the music, the pain from the twisted ankle abating, until I emerged from the forest onto a large, green lawn. A mansion, bigger than my family's castle, sat on the shoreline. Flowers of every size and color lined the walkway, and I followed the landscaped path to the backyard. The scent of the garden was like nothing I'd ever experienced before. Sweet and sensuous, whereas the ocean always reeked of fish and salt.

There were white marble columns and leather pool loungers. Maybe thirty people in their bathing suits were sipping drinks and writhing to the music. My pulse quickened—there were some young beauties. No one as gorgeous as Fiona, but some lovely women, nevertheless. I was used to admiring the curve of a tail but there was something very sexy about taunt human legs.

A sparkling infinity pool graced the edge of the beach, the Atlantic Ocean beginning where the blue of the pool ended.

A blonde-haired man with bleary eyes approached me. "I'm Chip."

"I'm Mira."

He looked at my feet, red and sore from my barefoot run down the mountain. "You need shoes." He slipped off his sandals. "I'll go get you a drink."

I put on the flip-flops and watched him stumble over to a granite bar. A woman in a white bathing suit strolled up. "Hi, I'm Gail. Who are you here with? This is a private party. *My* party." There was a hint of suspicion in her melodious voice, but I was too enraptured with her beauty to care. She had an imperious tilt to her chin as if she were royalty. The way Grandmother looked before her suspicious death.

My new legs felt weak as I gazed upon this vision of a woman. Her legs were laden with muscle and her curves were causing strange tingles in my new human parts.

"Well? Who invited you?" The vision asked again.

I stammered my answer, "Chip," while pointing to his broad, hairy back at the bar.

She frowned, tossing long black hair over one shoulder. "You're with my brother? I'd have thought you were out of his league. Far prettier than his usual skanks."

Chip staggered back and handed me a fizzy drink. I took a gulp and took a second to appreciate the deliciousness of the strawberry concoction. Much better than the horrid potion I'd drank earlier today.

Gail's hazel eyes were making my stomach flip. "She's with you?" she asked Chip.

"Ya, Mira's a babe," he slurred.

Gail appraised me and then nodded. "Help yourself to some food. Hey! They're playing my jam." She headed for the dance floor.

"Thank for the shoes." I danced around Chip and headed to the buffet table.

Along one side of the terrace was a long table laden with the most delicious morsels. There were oysters, shrimp, mussels, meat skewers, fruit salads, and even a fountain of sweet-smelling brown goo. My nose twitched with the waft of warm sugar and an undefinable yumminess. In Oceanus, there was plenty of seafood, but nothing that smelt or looked like this. I stuck my finger in the torrent of sticky sweetness and tasted it. It was rapturous.

Chip stumbled after me. "Hey, you need another drink?"

"No. But what is this heavenly food?"

"A chocolate fondue. What? You've never seen one before? Where are you from?"

I scowled at him. "Nowhere you've ever been." Chip was ruining my appetite. I tried to walk around him to the buffet table.

"Let's swim, hot stuff." Chip hoisted me up and twirled me toward the infinity pool. What was with these human men? They needed some time in our sea dungeon to teach them respect.

My muscles froze.

Must. Not. Get. Wet.

I struggled, but Chip was too strong. We both tumbled into the warm pool. I gasped as the water enveloped me.

Chip splashed and cheered. "Cannonball!"

My skin tickled. I kept my head under the water as the transformation began. Pressure as my legs turned to flippers. Frustration closed my throat. I hadn't even made it to Provincetown yet! What a waste of a spell.

Chip's hands slipped from my sides. "What the…"

The pool gallery became silent. All eyes were on me. Even the music stopped.

I bubbled, "No." I clenched my fists, and surfaced.

The first thing I saw were Gail's disbelieving eyes.

"Did someone spike the punch with acid?" Gail scratched her ear. "I think I'm seeing things."

Really? I thought. *She is more worried about her punch bowl than the actions of her despicable brother? Maybe the world above the waves is no better than Oceanus.*

Chip clambered out of the pool, shivering in shock. Without legs, I couldn't follow him up the ladder, so I swam the perimeter. My blood boiled as I rammed my fists into the sides of the fiberglass of the pool. I imagined Chip's face with every punch. Struggling to work up enough momentum, I launched myself over the edge of the infinity pool with my arms outstretched and dived toward the ocean.

I missed the water, landing with a solid *thunk* on the beach. Sand spewed up and rained onto my back. The surf I'd avoided earlier was now a glistening goal. There was a row of shocked faces in the backyard. Gail didn't look quite so beautiful with her mouth open in astonishment. This was a case of her insides not matching her outsides, and she could never be my true love. But I couldn't even worry about the witch's curse at this second. As a mermaid, I would die on land, so I concentrated on wiggling my body, pulling with my arms, and whacking my powerful tail. I was getting closer to the sea but finding it harder to breathe.

Chip hefted himself over the railing, dropped, and ran down the beach, staggering slightly. "Beautiful mermaid, I will come to help you!"

Just as his sister became uglier, Chip looked better to me in my eyes. Maybe not all human men were irredeemable. At least he was trying to save me now. How was he to know that throwing me into a pool would destroy my magical mission to find love?

Just as Chip's big hands grabbed my flipper, I reached the ocean. I wasn't sure how the drunk human man thought he was going to help me and, thankfully, I didn't have to find out. The tide timing was perfect, and his fingers slipped off me as I glided into the depths toward Oceanus. Swimming home, frustration mounted in my chest, creating a band of pain. Instead of my usual grace and speed, I swam like a sea turtle with a broken fin.

Slowly.

Awkwardly.

Hours later, the zombie worms of Endora's lair waved at me. The jagged teeth on the bony skull promised a grim welcome. I squinted. Fiona was waiting at the entrance, pulling at her mohawk. Checking my watch, I'd been gone for almost twenty-four hours. Minutes left before Endora had my swimming power forever.

When Fiona caught my eye, she swam over in a rush of bubbles.

Endora waved her tentacles from her lair. "Fiona, get back here! She knew the terms."

My watch was about to roll to noon. Fiona grabbed me in a hug.

"I should have stayed with you in Oceanus." She kissed my cheek. "Or you should have run away with me. We are stronger together! You've always been my true love."

My heart felt like it would burst out of my chest, but could I trust her? I pushed her off. "You sabotaged me. Why did you make me miss the boat?"

"I was going to meet you on that island! Tell you I loved you. But Endora figured me out and wouldn't let me leave!"

My heart filled with joy. Just like with Chip, I had misjudged Fiona. She wanted to help me, not hurt me. "I love you, too. I always have."

"Are we in time?" Fiona grabbed my wrist.

As the clock hand hit VII, strength flowed back into my flippers.

A huge smile lit up Fiona's face. We made it!"

I hugged her, but our celebration was short-lived. The water turned icy as Endora grabbed us, creepy long tentacles pulling us apart. "True love or not, you'll never be accepted in Oceanus. You both work for me now."

I whacked Endora with my tail. Fiona pulled out her long spoon and stuck it in Endora's eye.

Purple goo flowed into the water as Endora covered her injured face. She backed away, her mouth spewing hate. "You two are cursed. You deserve each other."

We watched as Endora slunk back into her lair, already muttering a healing incantation for her injured eye.

I took Fiona's hand. "I think it's time we taught King Dragonfish and all of Oceanus a thing or two about love."

"Oh, it's on." Fiona spun her spoon. "I've learned a few nasty spells working for Endora. We have some tools to oust your grandfather, if it comes to that."

We swam back to Oceanus to fight for our rights instead of fleeing or hiding.

The tide was turning. I would love whom I pleased. Fiona and I were stronger together.

About the Author

Angelique Fawns is a journalist and speculative fiction writer. She began her career writing articles about naked cave dwellers in Tenerife, Canary Islands. After selling her first story to EQMM, she fell in love with weird fiction, which is ACTUALLY stranger than non-fiction. You can find her lurking at @angeliquefawns on X, blogging about upcoming calls at www.fawns.ca, or gazing into the abyss hoping it stares back at her. Over 80 stories published. Find some in *Mystery Tribune*, *Amazing Stories*, and *Space & Time*.

Psalm of the Selkie

by

Morgan J. Muir

Psalm of the Selkie

*M*y love, stay with me, like this," he said as they embraced, and she gave him her skin on the cold Scottish shores. "Someday, my love, we will live by the sea," he promised. As he always did.

The years crawled by. Lumbering, like the cattle pulling the plow.

"I wish we could move back to the shores. I know how much you miss it," he soothed as he took her and their children farther inland.

Their children grew tall, and her soul grew thin.

"Would that we were free to visit the shores," he said with a quick kiss, then off to squander their meager funds, their children grown and flown.

And she was, again, alone.

The Selkie watched him leave astride their horse, braving the storm to drink with the men in the village tavern. What a stupid thing was money. She'd been free before. The winds beat against the wall, rattling the shutters, full of the scent of the moor. They were so far from shore that not even a hint of salt colored the storm.

She shut the door and turned back to their small home. A single room, with hearth, and stove, table and chairs. Where she had raised her sons to men. A loft bedroom above. For years, this had been her world. Cleaning, cooking, teaching, sewing, starving as she put food into the mouths of others. It encompassed her, dull browns and grays and greens.

She wiped her hands on her rough-spun apron. Her husband would expect a warm meal when he returned. Whenever that would be.

The wind burst open a shutter, teasing her long hair from its confines. It whispered to her of half-remembered dreams, and deliberately forgotten hopes.

Come back to me.

She closed her eyes and breathed in the scent. Memories washed over her. Flowing through the smooth, cool darkness. Eating when she chose, resting when she tired. Gleaming, silken silver and black. Whispers of sunlight and warmth and—

The Selkie slammed the shutter closed and shoved her flyaway hair back under the cap. She glimpsed her reflection. Her hair was dark and lackluster, the same as her eyes. There was no going back. She had chosen this. To be with a man she had loved. Settling her cap, she turned away. Her husband would be expecting his dinner.

Long after the storm had passed, and the moon lit the endless moor, her husband stumbled back through the door and dropped to the table with an expectant look.

"Anything interesting happen in town?" she asked, setting a bowl of stew before him with a chunk of bread.

"Just the usual nonsense." He dug into the food as though he hadn't eaten in a week. "There's a band of gypsies come to town with a freak show. You're to stay away from them, you hear?"

The Selkie nodded. Her stomach grumbled, but she would eat once he slept.

He held her hand a moment, looking up into her eyes. "You're a good woman, lass. I'm lucky to have ye."

She smiled and slipped her hand away. "I'll go take care of the horse."

The next morning, her husband left early to help at a neighbor's farm.

"Don't be going anywhere," he said, throwing his thick tartan around his shoulders. "I expect I'll be hungry when I return, and I'll be wanting a full meal."

She smiled up at him, and he kissed her. And again, she was alone. There was much to do. Their small farm had many chores, more now that her children were grown and she had no help. Her husband did not tolerate visitors.

Emptiness surrounded her. The dry, silent house bore down on her. Sucked the breath from her lungs. Gasping, she grabbed her threadbare cloak and flung herself through the door, into the wild, fresh air. Her feet carried her. Away. She had to get away. Anywhere.

She followed her feet as the sun rose higher into the sky. Strange sounds beckoned her. Pausing, the Selkie cocked her head. It was music, but a kind she had never heard before. Curious, she followed it until she caught sight of the gypsy caravan: a spray of wagons vibrantly colored like the sea at sunset, set into a circle. A crowd had gathered, and criers called out wares.

The Selkie hesitated. Her husband had told her not to. She bowed her head. She was bound to obey.

"Come, see the wonders!" the voice cried. "The boneless man! The bravest woman! Creatures never before seen, from the depths of the ocean!"

The Selkie hesitated. It had been years since she had seen so much as a fish. Perhaps just a look?

"Pretty lady!" A child grabbed her hand. His toothless smile reminded her of her sons at that age. His strange clothes were vibrant underneath a familiar boyish muddiness. "For just a bod, I'll give ya a tour!"

The boy pulled on her hand. Pulled on her heart. Would her sons have children soon? Would she ever see them again? The Selkie pulled a bodle from her pouch and allowed him to pull her toward the ring.

"Admission's fourpence," a gruff man said, stepping in front of her.

Her heart fell. That was more than she could afford.

"The pretty lady's given me a bod for a tour," the boy said, raising himself to his full height, which was barely to her waist.

"Is that so?" The man gave her a skeptical look. "For the pretty lady, then, twopence."

The boy gave her a hopeful look. She would have to go without for a while. But she had done so before. With a sigh, she fished out the price, and the man let her through.

The boy ran off, yammering. With a laugh, the Selkie made to follow, but a tune caught her ear. It entrapped her mind and snagged her soul.

The Selkie spun, looking for the source.

The young boy sighed and came back. "Everyone always wants to see *her,*" he pouted, taking her hand. "Come on, I'll take you."

He led her to a wagon surrounded by drapes. A hefty woman, with curling black hair held back by a coined shawl, barred the entrance. Another bodle exchanged hands, and the Selkie stepped through. The world around her fell still.

Inside the makeshift tent, a cage with a glass-bottomed tank sat within a staged wagon. The tank held seawater; the salt of it filled her nose like a stale whiff of the memory of home. Her knees nearly buckled as she greedily breathed it in. Memories pounded at her mind, demanding to be freed. It was too much. She nearly turned to run back out, to run home. Back to the life that was slowly killing her.

Gripping the child's hand, she stood straighter and looked past the tank and the bars to what lie within the greenish water. A long, scaled tail, too long to straighten in the tank, curled limply over itself. Delicate fins edged the tail in muted hues of greens and blues and silver. Moving her eyes up the tail, the creature's form changed gracefully into the slender waist, ribs, breasts, and upper body of a woman. A Siren.

The Selkie stepped forward. The Siren's arms, clinging to the bars for support, were edged with flowing, translucent fins. Scales traveled up her sides and neck, delicately framing her very human face. Her dark hair clung wetly to her body, past her waist to fan out across the water.

The Siren pulled herself farther out of the water.

"This is dangerous," the Selkie whispered.

"Naw," the boy said, a grin in his voice. "We cut out her tongue. Ain't nothing she can do without no tongue."

The Selkie moved forward again, transfixed by the Siren's dark eyes.

The boy ran forward and banged his stick against the bars. "Sing for the pretty lady!"

The Siren glared at the boy and lunged. He scampered backwards, falling into the mud below the tank. The Siren laughed, a weird, haunted laugh that twisted through the Selkie's spine. The boy scrambled to his feet and bolted out of the tent.

The Siren grinned, showing the Selkie her sharp teeth. Her laugh transformed into a quiet vocalizing. It moved, ebbing and flowing, like the waves on the beach. It pulled her forward, like the tide, and spoke of gliding, flying across the world, the sun on her back and the endless ocean below her. It snaked its way under the locked door in the Selkie's mind where she kept the hidden things. Things not to be remembered. Things like hope.

The Siren's wordless song cracked open the locked door, and the Selkie saw what was behind it.

And it *hurt*.

The Siren reached through the cold metal bars, stretching to touch her hand.

Sister.

Gasping, the Selkie turned and ran. She ran blindly. Towards home. The Siren's song haunted her as she tried to push the emotions away. Back to where she had kept them. Hiding away the pain that she could do nothing about.

But the Siren had *seen*.

Seen *her*.

Tears streamed down her cheeks as she began the monotony of her chores.

For the first time in years, she had been *seen*.

The Selkie stood atop a cliff. Below her roiled the stormy ocean, dark blues and frothy whites, calling to her as it battled the stony land.

Return to me.

She dreamed. She knew she dreamed. She had not seen the ocean since giving the man she loved, the man she trusted, her skin. He had hidden it from her as surely as he had hidden her from the ocean.

The storm lashed around her, the sting of freshwater shocked her skin. Exuberant, life affirming Joy filled her soul as she ran toward the cliff and dived. The air flowed around her as she flew, free, unbound, and wild, back into the deep embrace of home.

The Selkie woke. It was not yet midnight. She was in her home, beside her sleeping husband. The joy of the dream fled from her as quickly as it had come, leaving her empty. She had not felt joy like that since…

With a sigh, she slipped out of the bed. Since longer than she could remember.

The Selkie looked at her husband. She had loved him once. When he was a different man. Tonight, he had returned home tired, cranky, and complaining. The food wasn't what he wanted, the house wasn't tidy enough, why hadn't she fixed the leak in the roof? The Selkie had bowed her head, demurred, and promised to do better. He had smiled at her, and she had kept her true thoughts tucked away. Unseen.

He had done nothing to soothe the turmoil the Siren had stirred.

Wrapping her thin cloak around her shoulders, she slipped out into the rain. The wind cut her to the bone. Her simple, worn tartan could not keep the cold from her the way her own coat would.

At the gypsy camp, a few shapes still huddled around a fire, but the rest was still and silent. Only a fool or wild beast would be out in this weather. Which was she? The Selkie slipped through the shadows, making her way to the Siren's tank.

The Siren, huddling beneath the surface of the water, stirred and turned toward her. She reached out, pressing her hand against the glass. Slowly, the Selkie did the same. A smile lit the Siren's face, and she reached up, pulling her head and shoulders from the water and reached out.

Sister. The Siren's voice whispered against her mind.

Slowly, the Selkie lifted her hand, touching the Siren's

"Sister." The Siren's voice was now clear in her mind. "What are you doing so far from our home?"

Memories flashed before her, and the Selkie found herself responding with her first thought. "I was beguiled by a man who took me away." It was true, but the bitterness of it surprised her. Bitterness she had not allowed herself to feel these many years. The Selkie thought of the happy times with her children. Smother it. Don't feel. Don't feel.

The Siren smiled. "Much the same as myself, it would appear."

She tried to smile but failed. "No."

"You're telling me," the Siren said, cocking her head, "that you are not trapped, forced to perform for men, and have not had that which was most precious stolen from you?"

The Selkie pulled her hand from the Siren's grasp. "It's not like that," she whispered.

Is it not? The Siren's voice was softer, but still clear.

"This was a mistake." She turned to leave.

Please! Anguish colored the Siren's voice, matched by a small, strangled vocalization.

The Selkie's heart broke at the sound. She *knew* that sound.

Help me. Together, we can be free.

She closed her eyes. She couldn't. The force of the emotions held back for years pushed against the Selkie, breaking against her mind like the current against stones. She could be stone and withstand.

The ocean is not meant to be caged.

A tear slipped down the Selkie's cheek. Stone was never what she was meant to be. Taking a deep breath, she turned back. "How can I help?"

The Siren took her hand. "You must help me get away from this place."

"But how? I cannot pull your wagon. And even if I could, we would be noticed."

Deep green hair swirled through the water as the Siren shook her head. "Sister, I, too, am human on land. But my change takes time. I can free myself from the cage, but I can neither change nor travel quickly enough to escape."

The Selkie nodded. "I will bring the horse tomorrow night and carry you to my home. From there you'd be free."

"It is not enough. I do not understand life on land; I would be lost on my own." The Siren pulled herself closer to the bars, her face inches from the Selkie's. "But together we could both be free."

The Selkie's voice came out in a shaking whisper. "I cannot leave my husband."

"You cannot leave your skin."

She turned her head away in shame. Hiding from the truth was a thing of Men. She could not return to the water.

"I would never ask it of you," the Siren said, her eyes softening. "We must simply convince your man to take us there. And to bring your skin."

She sagged as the hope she hadn't realized she carried fled from her. "How? He does not listen to me."

"I will teach you a tune. You must sing it to him every time he is around, then whisper that which you would have him do."

"But I am no siren. My voice holds no power."

The Siren smiled her sharp smile. "It will have enough for this."

Cool sunlight broke over the distant hills, glancing off the dough the Selkie worked beneath her hands. She hummed her new tune cheerily, kneading the bread with its beat. Her husband thundered down the stairs, muttering as he pulled his shirt over his head.

"Quit that noise, hm? It's strange," he grumbled, taking a seat before the meal already laid out for him. "And ye've no business bein' strange."

The Selkie's voice caught in her throat. She kept her eyes down. She should have prepared better. He didn't like things to change. She had thought all night, trying to imagine a scenario where he would take her to the sea. Certainly not for her sake. She had tried everything over the years. Not to leave him, of course, but just for a break. A chance to be home. Just for a bit.

And how would she convince him to return her skin?

"…and young Mac can't be bothered to think about what he's doing, the fool," her husband complained between bites, and the Selkie nodded, making appropriately timed affirmations. "Just tries to do it all at once, never stoppin' to think things through. One step at a time, I always say…"

One step at a time. The phrase stuck in her mind. Such a human concept. In the water, life was about flow and direction. Life on land had taught her that such a mentality meant only one thing: getting stuck. As she had taught their children, she needed to take a first step. She took in a steadying breath and began to hum over her husband's complaints about her cooking and their lack of coin.

Softly she added words.

"And to the ocean they returned
To find the things of greatest worth."

His voice trailed off as he listened.

"And receive all that for which she'd yearned
When worn again her skin of birth."

"Here now, what's that you're singing?"

"Hm? Oh, it's just some old song I knew from before we met. I'd forgotten about it until that storm yesterday. Silly, I know." The Selkie resumed her song as her husband rose and donned his cloak and shoes.

"Yon trove for he who's swift and fly
The sleekit Selkie and the sky.
Gold and silver beneath the waves

And all the wealth ye'd ever crave."

She handed him a pack with his lunch and sent him off with a kiss. Perhaps this might actually work.

She sang softly as she worked, perfecting the words of her song. He found her mucking the barn when he returned home that evening, singing her gentle song.

"Alone he'd left her for a while
Another came who'd missed her smile.
Her lover's kiss brought back her gleam
And found again 'twas lost to dreams."

The Selkie fed the horse while he ate inside. As she returned to the house, he was already on his way out.

"Going to the tavern?" she asked. It was earlier than normal, but that worked in her favor. It meant he would be gone longer. "Will you be late?"

"No doubt," he said, giving her a quick embrace. "Keep my bed warm for me, eh?"

She smiled at him and watched until he had disappeared over the hill. How long before she could leave without being noticed?

Sunset, she decided.

In the fading light, the Selkie got the horse and set out. She rode quickly to the gypsy camp. Doubtless, he would be late. She would have time.

Sliding from the horse's back near the Siren's wagon, the Selkie dropped silently to the ground, and ducked through the drapes. The cage door swung open above a crumpled figure. The Siren perched above with a dangerous smile, her long tail moving slowly through the dark water.

"Did you kill him?" the Selkie asked, rushing forward.

Shh, the Siren responded in her mind. *We haven't much time before he is missed.* Her eyes gleamed in the darkness. *Hand him to me, and I will lock him in the cage he gave me.*

The hunger in her voice sent a chill through the Selkie. She shook her head. "I'll drag him beneath the wagon. Then we must go."

The Siren pursed her lips a moment, then nodded.

Once the body was moved—still warm and supple, the Selkie was relieved to note—she stood to let the Siren climb onto her back. The strong green arms tightened around her neck, pulling her back and pressing against her throat.

The Selkie gasped, pulling at them for air. "Not so tight! Killing me will not free you."

"Oh, right." The arms loosened a little, and the Siren leaned her head forward, shifting her weight onto the Selkie. "Apologies."

With a heave, the Selkie pulled forward, dragging the long tail out of the water. It flopped wetly on the ground, and the Siren cringed. The Selkie grit her teeth. Her burden was heavy, and the saltwater that soaked through her clothes burned worse than the rain. But she had carried worse for longer. Shoring up her own stubbornness, she dragged them both forward.

The horse snorted and pranced as they reached him, but stood fast. Loyal, he was.

The Selkie helped the Siren heave herself over his back, grasping the pack harness.

"Can you hold on, or should I tie you?" the Selkie whispered, as the Siren settled in, bent at the waist with her tail dragging along the ground on one side, and her hair along the other.

"I can hold on." Her eyes flicked to the circle of wagons. "Let's be gone."

The walk back took an eternity. The Siren's tail dragged in the dirt when she could no longer hold it up, and she grunted in quiet pain each time. They paused at every strange noise to strain for the sound of pursuit.

Just as she was sure they were clear, the Selkie's house came into view.

Light spilled from the windows. Her breath caught in her throat, choking her.

Her husband had come home early.

Swallowing, the Selkie squared her shoulders and continued forward. There was no other way but forward.

She hid the Siren in the empty stall and turned the horse loose in his box before her husband barged in, his voice already raised.

The Selkie stood before him, her head bowed, looking contrite at whatever it was he was screaming about. She really didn't bother to listen anymore. It was always the same. Probably about dinner and a cold house. He grabbed her shoulders and shook her. Anger flared in her soul. His words broke through her disconnect.

"… leaving at who knows where at all hours! Sneaking around, as if I wouldn't know. Are ye seeing another man?"

"No," the Selkie protested weakly.

"You're lying!"

Lightning seared through her face and skull, and she found herself on the ground. Dirt and rough straw scratched at the side of her face that was not stinging. The Siren's face lay inches from hers, the anger in her eyes a reflection of her own.

Tame not the ocean, o fool.

The Selkie looked away.

He had hit her.

He had never hit her.

She needed to rise before he found the Siren. Gathering herself, the Selkie pulled herself to her feet. She glanced at his eyes, but looked away before he could see her rage.

Use the song, the Siren urged.

Softly, she responded, adding a quiet lilt to her voice. "I have never been unfaithful to you."

"Of course you haven't." Her husband softened. "I got an offer today from a business partner. No, no one you have heard of. But I will be gone for some time. It will involve some sailing, you see."

Her mind raced, but she nodded calmly, and she took his hand. "Let's discuss this inside."

He allowed her to lead him back to the house as he described details. The details didn't matter to her. She had to convince him to take her along.

"I will be leaving first thing in the morning."

What if he didn't agree to take her? Maybe she could just follow behind? Would he send her back? What of her skin? And what of the Siren?

When she didn't respond, he reached out to her, stroking the side of her face that didn't hurt, and knocked away some of the straw that still clung to her flyaway hair. "I am sorry."

She patted his hand gently. "How could I possibly be upset?" She looked out the window with a wistful smile. "I'm sure I'll find a way to pass the time. Perhaps visit an old friend."

Her heart pounded. Would he take the bait? Had it been enough?

"Or you could come with me."

She gave him the most charming smile she possessed. One, she was surprised to find, was nearly genuine. Once again, she added the soft lilt to her words. "I would love that."

The next morning, they set out. Him, astride the horse, with a large, expensive cloak she had never seen carefully bundled behind him and tied securely atop a pack of simple supplies, and the two women on foot. The Siren looked back at the home she had lived in for far too long. There were many good memories there: children's laughter, stories sitting around the warm fireplace, happiness. Despite all the pain, there *had* been happiness.

"Hey, come along!" her husband called back to her, teasing in his voice. "You waiting for someone?"

"Of course not," she said with a smile. She shouldered her own pack and caught up.

As they walked, she glanced at the Siren walking beside her. She had shed her tail in a process the Selkie knew better than to ask about. The fins and scales had faded, leaving her the appearance of a slender young woman, a half-starved wisp of a girl, really. Her lanky black hair fell to her waist, and the Selkie had done what she could to help her brush and pin it earlier that morning. She had brought the Siren an old dress, faded enough that her husband likely wouldn't remember it, that had long been overdue for the scrap pile. Without shoes, the Siren winced at each step of her fresh, tender feet. The Selkie would have to help her bind them when they stopped for lunch.

The Selkie's husband gestured her forward, and she hastened to catch up to him, clutching the strap of her own heavy pack.

"Who is that woman again?"

"Mac's cousin's daughter, don't you remember?" The Selkie touched his leg as they walked. "A poor young widow, with not a bod to her name. His wife asked us to help her some months ago, and she only just arrived."

Her husband huffed. "Don't see why she had to come along. Coulda stayed and watched the house."

"But she'll be so much more useful with us, here. You'll be far more comfortable with her to help me."

Her husband sniffed. "Sing me that song again, would you? I think it would help to pass the time."

"Of course."

The days slid into each other, like rain on a windowpane. At night, the women built a fire and cooked whatever the Selkie's husband caught for them. The Selkie made sure her husband caught her glancing back the way they had come. The cold rainy weather sent a chill through them, and the fire dried their skins. When the Selkie insisted that the other woman would freeze to death in the night without at least a cloak, her husband wrapped himself in the elegant fur-lined cloak and told her to share hers with the Siren.

Each night, she hummed the man to sleep with whispered lines of the Siren's song. The fourth morning, when the Siren joined in as they broke camp, her husband took her aside.

"I thought she was mute."

The Selkie shook her head. "Her husband was a brute. He cut out her tongue for telling folks he'd beaten her."

"You sure she's not...related to you?"

The Selkie gave him a reassuring squeeze of the arm. "I swear to you on all I hold dear, I had never seen her before a few days ago."

Her husband searched her eyes. "You wouldn't lie to me?"

"How could I lie to you? You hold that which is most precious to me."

"Your heart?" He touched the cloak, wrapped tightly on the back of his saddle. A task he would not allow her to help with.

She smiled at him again and started down the road.

By the sixth day, she could smell the ocean. On the seventh day, as the sun neared the western horizon before them, they crested a hill, and there it was. The Selkie's knees buckled, and the Siren slipped under her arm, steadying her. Her heart screamed at her to drop the pack, her burdens, her past, and run to the open embrace of home.

An embrace that would kill her without her skin.

"You could go," she whispered to the Siren. "There is nothing holding you back."

The Siren glanced to the husband, and bit her lip. "I promised to help you get your skin back."

The Selkie nodded and stood on her own. The wind of the oncoming storm pulled at her cap. "We'll get my skin and leave him behind."

If you insist. The Siren began her soft hum, a different tune than she had taught the Selkie, and they continued forward.

Dark gray and blue waves crashed on the shore as they neared. The Selkie's husband had them wait for him while he secured a small boat. The sunset, through the stormy clouds, gilded the world as they waited.

"I've always loved the colors," the Selkie said, sitting on a log and digging her sore, tired feet into the cold sand. "The surface world is so much more vibrant."

"Only up here. Where I am from, the water is warm and clear, and life is far more colorful."

The Selkie's husband called to the women from down the beach. Obligingly, they came. The wind again tore at the Selkie's cap, and she held it down. A man stood nearby, holding the rope to a small fishing boat with a single sail. Small enough to be managed by a single man, but large enough to brave the choppy water.

"There's a storm coming in," the fisherman said, giving a knowing look to the sky. "Whatever it is you're meaning to do, you'd better wait until morning,"

The Siren's subtle song increased, carried along the wind in a haunted tune.

The fisherman glanced sharply at her, his face paling. His mouth worked, but no sound escaped. He turned from them, tripping over his feet, and ran.

"I wonder what got into him," the Selkie's husband said. He shrugged and turned to his wife, throwing the heavy cloak over his shoulders. "I'm going out to find this treasure. You two stay here with the horse and wait for me."

146

Panic filled the Selkie's chest. He couldn't leave with her skin. "The storm is frightful. Leave your fine cloak with me so it doesn't get ruined."

He pulled it tighter. "It's far colder on the water than here. I will need it more."

The Siren's song pushed at her. She gathered her wits. Wistful smile. Act happy about this. "I understand. I'll take the horse and head back to the last village we passed." She began walking away from him, allowing her cap to fall carelessly away, freeing her hair. "There was an inn there, a wonderful place to meet."

He grabbed her arm and pulled her back. "You *have* been lying to me! There is someone following us! You've meant for me to go out in this storm and die so you can be with your lover. Don't deny it!"

"Then take me with you!" she shouted back, pressing her body against his. She slipped her hand up his chest and under the cloak. The soft fur that lined it sent lightning through her arm. "Do as you've always promised and take me back!"

"You've no right to be telling me what to do." He grabbed her hand roughly away and shoved her into the boat.

The Siren already sat at the bow, huddling beneath the Selkie's cloak to keep the spray from changing her. Her song continued, just audible above the rising wind.

Grumbling, the man shoved the small boat into the water and jumped in. Settling himself, he rowed them out into the depth, toward the fading sunset. He moved to the beat of the Siren's song, taking them farther and farther out as the waves grew wilder. The Selkie held to the mast of the small boat with white knuckles, a lantern swinging overhead. The spray burned her skin as the shore disappeared behind them.

The Siren's song modulated. *Ask him,* she said. *Ask him again for your skin.*

"Please," the Selkie said, crawling carefully toward her husband, the saltwater soaking through her clothes, burning like a hand on an oven. He slowed his rowing and looked at her with vacant eyes. "It is cold. Share your cloak with me."

He cocked his head, as though confused. Mechanically, his hand unlatched the cloak, and he held it out to her. The Siren's song continued as the Selkie snatched it from him, falling back beside the other woman.

She turned the cloak inside out, her hands caressing the soft black fur. Tears streamed down her face, choking her as she inspected the thing that he had made from her skin. She gasped, feeling the seams where he had cut it and sewn it back together to fit his will. Not the shape of her at all.

The Siren watched, realization dawning in her eyes. She slipped her hand into the water, her long claws forming instantly on her wet hand, and she began tearing at the seams that held the skin to the heavy tartan.

The Selkie's anguished cry cut through the darkness as the Siren stripped away the seams.

The man lunged at his wife, his hands grasping for the cloak.

The Siren surged forward, raking his face with her claws. Rage filled his eyes as he grabbed her arm away, swinging wildly at her, and knocking her down.

Behind them both, the Selkie tore at the remaining seams, tearing ragged bleeding wounds through her own hide.

The Siren screamed and again launched herself at the man before he could turn back to his wife. Clinging to his back, she twisted her arms around his neck, tightening with what strength she could. He reached back and grabbed her hair, tearing her arms from his neck. She glanced to the Selkie who sat, smearing her blood against the edges of the raw fur, binding them back together.

"You contemptuous whore!" the man screamed, flinging the Siren from him. Her back cracked against the wooden side, and she grunted, attempting to roll onto her stomach as her legs slipped into the frigid water. He grabbed her hair again, heaving her overboard. "I'll teach you to interfere!"

He pushed her head beneath the water, the glow of the lamp casting disfiguring shadows across her face. She clung to his arm, scratching and frantic, and he pulled her up. She sputtered and struggled as she faked trying to catch her breath. The Siren cast a glance to the Selkie who stood, her bloody pelt now scarred, but whole. The boat rocked wildly beneath them.

Now is your chance!

"Let him go," she whispered.

The Siren hesitated.

Seeing her glance, the man let go of the Siren and, with a roar, again went for his wife. Swift as a creature truly in its element, the

Siren grabbed hold of his arm, pulling him back. He looked down at her, contempt and disgust on his face at her cold touch. Lightning flashed, and for a single horrifying moment, he saw an achingly beautiful face below the surface, smiling with a predator's teeth and swirling hair that framed her features like death.

Panicked, he thrashed bracing himself against the side of the boat as the Siren pulled his arm slowly, unrelentingly, into the water. He reached for his wife. "Help me!"

She watched silently, slipping calmly from her dress.

"Wasn't I good to you?" The boat tipped as he struggled to pull back from the darkness "Save me, please!"

She loosened the laces of her corset, allowing it to drop to the wooden boards.

"Make her stop. I know you can!"

Her chemise fell in a pile at her feet.

"Please. Let's just go home."

The ocean must be free, the Siren's voice drifted to her.

She gave him a sad smile and draped her skin across her shoulders. "I am home."

The Siren reached up, grabbing his hair, and heaved him into the water.

The Selkie turned away, lifted the hood over her hair, and slipped into the water.

Free.

About the Author

Morgan J. Muir has always loved telling stories, especially stories with magic, hardships, and—eventually—happy endings. She is working hard on becoming a crazy cat lady and on curating her collection of hobbies. Morgan lives with her family in Utah.

You can find more of her work at morganjmuir.com and on FB @MorganJMuir

The Bottom of the World

by

Jayrod P. Garrett

The Bottom of the World

*E*very day at the water's surface, I listen to my sister Sirens ring their multi-tonal singing bowls. Feel the vibrations ripple through both the water and my floating body. Enjoy the yellow sun's warmth on my dark skin and black silksteel dress. Revel in the flight of white and red birds in the cerulean sky.

Or at least I did. These days, it's just noise while my body tremors drown out the healing vibrations. The sun's heat feels blistering, and I struggle to absorb the beauty of any colors because it all overwhelms me.

I often ask myself why? Is it abandonment? The death of my parents? Crippling anxiety? Yes, but no. Emptiness fills me. Better known to us merfolk as the Deeps

I raise a trembling, brown hand out of the water, remembering when I played the bowls, too. They say I'm a better Siren than my mom was. That it is good I didn't follow my father in being a Waveguard. But now I can't help any merfolk keep the Deeps at bay. Instead, I suffer from the worst case of the Deeps my clan's known in a decade.

Knowing if I remain much longer, some well-meaning merfolk will try to help me, I dive to set my body right again. It's only fifty meters or so; yet the lack of light allows me to calm myself. Except, now the worst part of my condition takes over again as my departure from the light blinds my eyes to color as well.

My fellow merfolk swim around me wearing colors vibrant and beautiful—but their silksteels are gray, their scales are gray, and their faces are gray. I look at my own gray hands and, not for the first time, I wish I could die. The problem with that is that the Deeps don't give you the will to die.

I swim down and pass too many people who call my name. Asking Marle this. Or Marle that. But why respond to the people grief erases from your mind?

A hand touches my shoulder. "Come to lunch with me. I miss you."

I turn to see a young merman with long hair, rows of scales set as armor underneath his silksteels, long legs, and eyes that I think once did something to me. He's said we had combat classes together before my father died. I wonder did he and Mother encourage me to become a Siren when Father passed?

"It's me. Antoine."

I'm sure he knows to tell me this because I've said I can't remember who he is too many times. I don't know why he bothers. What value do I have now? I swim away.

He grabs my wrist. "I can't keep doing this, Marle. I know it's been hard since your mom died. But please just respond. Tell me you hate me. Or that I annoy you. Or that you don't want to see me anymore. Don't just swim away. Again."

I should smile and tell him, "It's not you. It's me." Or tell him to try again tomorrow. Or maybe that looking at him reminds me of how empty I am. Instead, I pull my wrist free and swim away.

Down farther, roughly one hundred meters, a merkid swims through our village, delivering news about the safe escape of Lenni, a nearby village's Siren, as an elven ship had wrecked against her sounding bowls and stones. I laugh because if the elves won't wear their earplugs around Sirens, they deserve to die.

Though, my mother died thirty-five days ago in the first accident with the elves. This makes the fourth since then. I wish the other Sirens had died, too, and my heart catches in my throat at the thought. I swallow the emotion, and it dissolves like salt.

It's not a long swim to the large, reflective, house-bubbles where my clan lives. Our Bubblesmiths shape them with a thick soap that repels everything but the scale signature of a specific family. They are chained together with braids of seaweed to keep our homes together as a single community. I'm lucky mine is on the outer rim in our village. Otherwise, I'd probably float away before I could get home. It's so tiring to lie in the sun and shake.

As I lay my hand against the membrane of my bubble to settle in for another day of staring at the wall, I see a light brown, scaleless woman with fuchsia octopus tentacles instead of legs. I double take at her realizing I can see color and my whole body relaxes. Then I stare astounded at her voluminous electric pink curls. I've never seen hair like that before. Her eyes catch mine, and she swims up to me in an instant.

She pushes me back from my bubble, leans in close, and tilts her head back and forth. It makes her hair bounce in such a lovely way. Between her innocent nudity and beauty, I can't help a smile. The joy breaks at the memory of the elders reprimanding me. "You selfish little fool. How dare you feel pleasure looking at a Feral? They'll eat you."

She takes my hand and intertwines her fingers in mine. She grins. A mouthful of shark-like teeth shine at me, brilliantly white, and I'm lost in fear. This is a Feral Pactborn, someone who failed to keep her humanity after making a pact with an Elemental. I've heard stories of them ripping merfolk apart with claws or magic. And I realize she could kill me with a single bite. I pull away.

Her tentacles sweep me into a soft, yet firm hug. Warmth rushes through my body and I can see us in the reflective silver lining of my bubble. I struggle to free myself, but she takes my red hair in her hands and begins braiding it. In a singsong voice, she says, "You look worse than I did when I left. I'm glad I came back now."

I push back just enough to look at her face. Really look at her. Though the pink hair and light brown skin are new, the curves of her face, the blush of her cheeks, and her familiar hands are unforgettable. "Benate?"

She smiles and releases me. "Looks like I retained enough of myself for you to remember me."

I hug her as emotions roil through me. Anger, joy, fear, delight, sadness, and relief assault me in waves. My stomach flips, my mind races, and my skin tingles. For someone who struggles to recognize any of their emotions, this is the best kind of overwhelming.

I cup her face in my hands. Our foreheads touch. I want to dwell in this moment. There's so much to say. Too much that's happened. I thrust her back and slap her.

"Where were you?"

She rubs her cheek. "I deserve that. I should have come home sooner."

"I thought you'd never come home, sis. You left four years ago. We said your name in our village prayers for two years. And now you—" I hug her again. My eyes sting as they leak freshwater into the saltwater. "You better not leave again."

She holds me in her tentacles and lifts my face with her hand. "I came home because I heard about Mom. I'm so sorry I wasn't here for you."

For the first time I can remember, I cry. Not just cry. I sob. Blubber. I'm a mess. And it feels rejuvenating.

"You know that black is not your color. You should be wearing yellow. It complements your scales much better."

I summon my indigo-violet scales covering my legs to my arms to examine them. While most people know merfolk can move their scales into a tail or armor on their bodies, the secret we keep from the rest of the world is that we craft tools and weapons with our scales. It makes life among dangerous fish, squid, and crustaceans safe. I shape my scales into a sound bowl mallet for the first time in weeks and shake my head. "I forgot I could even do this."

My sister laughs. And it's like putting my ear against a sound bowl, full of vibration, vitality, and vibrance.

She rubs a hand along the scales on my arms and up my shoulders. "These make you special. Don't forget them."

"I won't." I wave at her new body. "What is it like having tentacles? Don't you miss your scales?"

She smiles and her shark-like teeth gleam like the sun. "I do, but I've spent most of the last four years in the sky. This is the deepest I've been in the water since I made my pact."

My eyes widen. "But you have tentacles!"

She laughs again and takes my hands in hers. "When I'm above the water, I have wings instead of tentacles. The best part is, I don't get the Deeps anymore, Marle."

How in the world did she free herself from the Deeps?

A low voice interrupts us. "Back away from her, Feral, and nothing will happen to you."

I turn to see Antoine and a group of hunters swimming in the water behind us. He shapes his scales from armor into a harpoon and others carry scale-formed tridents, spears, and cutlasses. I place myself between them and Benate. "This is my sister. Please don't hurt her."

Antoine's golden eyes narrow, and I remember losing myself in them before. "She may have been your sister." He pulls back his harpoon to his cheek. "But she's dangerous now. Just look at her teeth."

Benate says, "Antoine. You know me. I taught you how to use a harpoon."

Antoine and his crew fall back as if Benate screamed at them. I turn to look at her. "What just happened?"

She frowns. "They can't understand me. There's too much fear in for them to hear me instead of the terror of my Elemental." She grabs my hand and plunges us rapidly into the depths. "We don't have much time. Once I leave you, the Deeps will claim you again."

"Can't I just go with you?"

"I don't live in the ocean anymore, love. I came here to save my family. You are too precious to lose like so many of our kin."

She speaks true. I recall more than twenty names in the past two years alone we are mourning for. Folks we expected lost themselves to the Deeps. And holding her hand, I don't want to be one of them.

"What do I do?" I ask.

"Find Azure the Sprite. If you bond with her, our family—"

Benate screams as a harpoon pierces her back. The spines of its blade protrudes from between her breasts. White blood floods the water around us. Her blood is white? How many differences do Ferals have from us?

She lets go of my hand. "Dive. It's the only way to save—" She's ripped back through the water as Antoine recalls the harpoon.

I shift my scales into a purple scythe and start towards her, and then stop. Emptiness floods me as the mermen attack my sister. For all their claims of how dangerous she is, she doesn't fight back as their blades slice off her tentacles and fill the water with her blood. She blurs in the water as her tentacles form into legs once again and her arms shift into fuchsia wings. With a single flap, she jets towards the surface and vanishes from view.

Antoine swims towards me. His eyes are gray again. My mind races. Are Ferals dangerous? Will I become like my sister if I become one with an Elemental? Can I even make the trip down to where Azure lives? She's at the bottom of the sea. What if—

"Are you okay, Marle?" Antoine pulls me into his arms. His body heaves from the exertion of attacking my only family. His scales stained white with her blood. I look into his cold eyes and realize I don't want what is there. If he could hurt someone as beautiful as my sister, I never really knew him.

I shove him away and concentrate. My scales shift around my legs in a cyclone of motion. They spiral, weaving into a tail nearly twice as long as my legs. A dorsal fin and an anal fin both appear, running down to the taper of my tail where it transforms into what should be a dazzling yellow fluke, but is instead gray. It pushes me into a dive into the depths.

I think Antoine calls after me. He doesn't follow. Only those who want to feel so badly they are willing to die make this dive.

Three hundred meters down, the light is quite dim. Fish of various sizes swim around me. Gray, flat, and colorless, they are uninteresting to look at. Though they help me gauge my sight for between twenty to twenty-five meters. I dive deeper.

Six hundred meters down, forward is the only motion. I dodge fish at breakneck speeds, despite not knowing where this energy comes from. I only know I have to keep moving. To stop is to pause. To pause is to die. To die is to never feel anything again.

Nine hundred meters down, I can't see anymore. Thankfully, there seem to be fewer fish though. I've struck a few of them yet kept my momentum. They seem to be swimming upwards, which doesn't make sense until a strong current snatches me. I thrash as the water drags me into a whirlpool.

I flail against the current. I swirl into the current. It spins me helplessly in circles. Panic should rise in my chest. Fear should drive me on. But the numb of emptiness is swallowing me faster than the whirlpool. Why am I fighting? Is it even worth my time? At least, this way the ocean will kill me.

I hit something. Pain fills me. Sensation ripples through my limbs and my mind clears. I recall the village elders of telling our clan to never dive too far, because it's too dangerous. Are they right?

Benate speaks to my mind. "Forget them. You know how whirlpools work. You aren't helpless. Make a choice. Decide what you want."

I shake my head, curious how Benate spoke to me, but aware she's right. I need to focus. Make a choice? I can't swim. But I want—no, I need to get to Azure. I want to feel again.

I stop resisting, allow my body to relax and go limp in the water. The whirlpool carries me down and out through its center.

I'm out. I think this is where I should whoop, holler, or cheer. But instead, I drift downward. My limbs droop in the water and I drop towards the ocean floor. A crushing drowsiness makes sleep sound good right now.

Something pokey and hard cuts my stomach. I reel back in pain and realize I can't see. A memory of Father teaching me about bioluminescent sight in the depths comes to mind, and I pluck two scales from my tail. Opening one eye, I push a scale onto it and scream. He didn't tell me it would burn like laying on the land and drying your scales out. The pain doesn't subside before I push the second scale into my other eye. As my vision restores itself, I can see for a few meters in front of me. I look down and gasp.

Bodies line the ground. I've recited their names in prayer for the past four years. Celeste the Bubblecrafter, Melchior the Justice, Robrieght the Silksmith, Vivienne the Botanist, and Father.

Father. I swim towards his body. It's nothing like I imagined. Something ripped out his insides, leaving only a shell of his skin and scales behind. I don't know how this is even possible, but I can't bear to look at him. It's too much.

I remember Mother coming back to our bubble four years ago to tell us that Father wasn't coming home. He'd gone out to fight against a pod of killer whales that attacked our village and he'd been killed. Why did Mother and the elders lie about Father? What really killed him? Did he still die a protector?

I still dream of being like my father. To fight against powers bigger than me. To make my world safe. To laugh in the face of danger. Only I hadn't. Like a coward, I stopped learning to fight and learned instead to ring the sounding bowls like Mother. Now, by failing him, I also failed Mom.

What is that gray stuff in the water?

Blood is in the water. My blood. I feel at my stomach, and I realize I'm bleeding. With this realization, a series of tail scales swirl up and cap off the wound. Then all my scales flare as something within cries danger. A feeling familiar, but long forgotten.

I glide through the water, noticing multiple bodies half eaten. Others mere limbs. I close my eyes and search for vibrations around me.

I dodge to the left, just in time to evade a lumen shark. Its skin's bioluminescence is dim in the water, yet combined with the smell of my blood, it knows exactly where I am. Its teeth remind me of Benate. Only I know, unlike her, it will tear me apart. I swim away.

Another darts in from the left. I feel it before I see it. I swirl in the water to dodge it.

I swim as fast as I can. But they are faster.

I dodge one. Duck another. A third rushes in, behind the one I dodged, to sink its teeth into my stomach.

One I can handle. Two is difficult. Three is a death sentence. But pain offers life. I rip the one on my stomach off with my bare hands and move scales from my tail to close the wound.

Realizing I can't outswim three, I pull my scales away from my legs and shift them to places on my body just before they bite. I dart past one bite, block another, swerve to force another to miss, only to have another shark bite into my thigh.

Agony lights up my brain. I wouldn't survive many bites like this. Maybe not even these. Would I end up another body at the bottom of the sea?

"Azure knows what happened to Father," Benate says.

Hearing her voice reminds me why I came down here. Of what I can do. In a swarm of motion, I gather my scales and transform them into a scythe and slice off the face of the shark that's bitten me.

Gray blood fills the water and the sharks frenzy. Only now, our roles are reversed. I spin and cut, dash and slash, swirl and swish, cleaving the three sharks into pieces.

My gills flare behind my ears. It's been years since I last fought anyone. Pain echoes in my leg as I pry the jaws of the shark from my leg. I seal off the wound using the scales I'd made into a scythe. I didn't even think I could move like that anymore. I smile as I look at my crimson blood in the water mixing with that of the sharks. Was giving up fighting part of why I succumbed to the Deeps?

The ocean vibrates around me. I see nothing, yet the turbulence that swirls around me says something is happening.

"Come, child. You've done well to make it this far," a voice booms into my head. "The tunnel of water in front of you will lead you to my lair."

I reach a hand forward. Indeed, the water is shifting in unnatural ways, like a mini whirlpool. I question if I'll remain merfolk after this. But it doesn't stop me. I need to feel far too much to stop now. I dive into the water tunnel, and I'm swept down into a cave I couldn't see before.

I swim out of the current and into a golden haze marking this as the home of an Elemental. The haze opens up to a huge room with sapphires hanging from the ceiling, a floor of sky-blue larimar, and an obsidian table with Father lying atop it. I rush to him and check his gills to discover they still push water. He's alive, but dark skin is pale, his scales are in haphazard places all over his body covering wounds, and a large cut that sits underneath his ribs has been cleaned, salved, and wrapped in seaweed.

Laying a hand on his chest, tears leak into the water. My mind races with questions: How is he here? What did I see in the ocean? Why are there so many secrets? But I can only verbalize one. "Why are you here, Father?"

"Perhaps that's a question I can answer." Floating in the center of the room is a tiny blue woman, at most fifteen centimeters tall, with black braids twice as long as her body and a white dress made of slivers of shark teeth.

"Welcome. My name is Azure." She floats in the water, with a serene expression on her face, twinkling back and forth between turquoise and teal light. "I am the water Elemental of the Kulan Ocean. You've done well to reach me. I haven't had a visitor for four years now. Your father was the last."

I ball my hands into fists. She is responsible for everything that happened. Father didn't die. Which meant Benate didn't need to leave. Mother and I didn't have to mourn. Perhaps worst of all was that Mother didn't have to die. "You ruined my life."

"Good. You're feeling again, aren't you?"

I glare at Azure. "Of course, I'm feeling. You destroyed my family."

Azure sits down on my father's chest. "Tell me about that, dear. Tell me how I destroyed your family."

"The elders said Father died in a whale attack. If he didn't die, then my sister wouldn't have gotten the Deeps and run away. I would have chosen to remain a warrior, and I could have saved Mom."

"What would you have done, Marle?" Her eyes twinkle. I want to rip them out of her head. It wouldn't be hard, as small as she is.

"I could have fought. I could have stopped that ship."

"You're telling me you can stop a freighter full of elven goods with your scales?" Azure laughs. "That sounds like a fantasy, dear."

I lunge at her, and she blips out of existence to appear on my shoulder. "I don't think you are capable of hurting me anymore than you would be capable of stopping a ship. Though there is something you can do here. If you are willing to listen."

I don't want to listen to anything she has to say. I want to swim back home. Maybe invite Antoine down here to stab her. Except she glides from my shoulder to lay a tiny hand on my father's chest. "I know you came here to escape the Deeps. Most do, honestly.

"Only your father didn't. He came because he wanted to make a better life for you and your sister."

"How would any of this make a better life for us?" I blurt.

"He made a covenant with me to give his life to make certain you and Benate never suffered from the Deeps."

"So you didn't keep your promise?" I growl. "Some Elemental you are. I've wasted my time."

"No, after your mother died, he couldn't fulfill his end of the promise. Seems like you aren't the only one who thinks they can stop an elven—" She paused. "Warship."

Her words cut my rage away. "An elven warship?"

She pinches the bridge of her nose. "Yes. Warship. Grief-stricken, he abandoned his covenant with me to protect the Sirens of four other villages." Clenching her tiny fists, she kicks his chest softly. "I'm not heartless, girl. I allowed him to do so, but that's why you got the Deeps after your mother died. Protecting Sirens isn't what he promised me. And now he's destroyed his body to the point our bond is broken. He is no longer fit to do anything with me other than breathe. Unfortunately, he's doing a poor job of that."

I pause. Maybe Azure isn't what I thought she was. Still, I ask, "Why did my sister get the Deeps, then?"

"Marle, an Elemental pact takes time to be in force. By the time he completed his pact, your sister had already made a pact with my sister, Damini. They dwell in the sky together."

I hate to admit it all makes sense now. I cup my father's face in my hands and look him over again. It's clear she's been keeping him alive all this time by sheer force of will. As pale as he's become and with the amount of wounds he's sustained, he should be dead. "Why did you bring me here?"

She apparates in front of me. "I need someone to fulfill a covenant with me. Stopping the ships isn't the answer. More will come."

"What was his covenant with you, Azure?"

"To protect the Kulan Ocean. Not your people. Not Elementals. All the ocean."

I stroke his bald head. I think of all I've sacrificed to come here. "Can you save him?"

"Only within a covenant. My power is limited by your choice. If you choose to no longer suffer from the Deeps, then he'll die. If, however, you choose to save him, you'll continue to live afflicted with the Deeps."

I stare at the tiny woman. I can save my family or save myself. I hate her for making me make this choice. But not as much as I'll hate myself if I don't make it. How much of this did Benate know when she sent me? Maybe I hate her, too.

"Please save him."

Azure reaches her tiny hand up and the cavern above us opens to the entire ocean. Spirals of blue cords suffuse her body. Vibrant indigo, noble royal, cerulean, sky, cobalt, and ultramarine coalesce into her hands, where she holds all of it a moment before she touches my forehead.

Suddenly her chambers aren't only blue. Sapphires, emeralds, and rubies float in the chamber without a ceiling. Coral of red, orange, and yellow appears where once I'd seen mirrors. The ocean itself stratifies, and I can see the green hue of the depths and the speckles of salt dancing within the waves. I blink to see it all better and notice Azure is gone.

But the ocean swirls around me and suddenly rushes into my mouth. I can taste the salt and the flavor of fish beyond my wildest dreams. Savory flavors delight my tongue, leaving no breath to scream with as my gills flare, and I can hear the song of the ocean, an exhilarating tune that whispers to those with ears to hear that life is not meant to be lived beneath the waves alone.

The ocean fills my wounds, cleansing and healing them. Multiplies my shimmering indigo and violet scales from the hundreds into the thousands. Though I can't see her, I can feel Azure within me radiating warmth. She whispers, "Show us the ocean, Marle. I want to see it all through your eyes."

I gasp and look up not to darkness, but a vibrancy of color I'd never imagined. Above me, a silverback whale is diving with merfolk, of varied shades of brown, tan, and peach, upon it. Their garments of pink, red, yellow, green, blue, violet, and purple iridesce in the light of the water. Above them I see millions upon millions of fish, swimming in every direction in more colors and shades than I even comprehend.

I see Antoine and his crew in our village outside the bubbles of the elders, crying. His golden eyes don't attract me anymore, as I realize I am someone he'd kill now.

My breath catches as the Sirensong echoes in my ears. It vibrates through my body, and I feel every inch of my body alive like never before. The warmth of the sun fills my chest. I exhale a breath. How did I live without this? I can even see the red and white birds flying through cerulean skies.

But my vision doesn't end there. I look farther and see a light brown woman in a marvelous mint green dress that complements her huge fuchsia wings. Her voluminous pink hair bounces as she soars through the sky.

A hand lands on my shoulder as Father stands beside me. "Thank you. You've made our family whole again."

About the Author

Jayrod P. Garrett believes in working towards a world where all of us can feel we belong. They are a storytelling educator with a Masters of Fine Arts in Creative Writing from the University of Nevada, Reno. As a child, they came to Utah on a three-week vacation that became more than forty years. During that time, they transitioned from being a faithful member of the Church of Jesus Christ of Latter-Day Saints into a nonbinary, Black, atheist, U.S. Veteran with PTSD and ADHD. Currently they are a stay-at-home parent with a slash career where they teach Black students about Black history with RISE Virtual Academy, tell stories for the Nubian Storytellers of Utah Leadership, run role playing games at Salt Lake City's Legendarium, and build community with writers as the Belonging Coordinator of Superstars Writing Seminars. They live in northern Utah with their spouse and three children. You can find more on their work, their writing journey, and where they are teaching at jayrodpgarrett.com.

Tin Man

by

D. H. Aire

Tin Man

The crew thought showing *The Little Mermaid* was funny the night before. I would have shuddered if I weren't made of steel, locked in position on the bridge, listening on sonar as *Nautilus Six* passed over the shattered remains of the toppled spire that once was the Washington Monument.

Twisted metal and concrete littered the underwater landscape of the city I harvested. It was as abandoned as I was, the last man aboard *Nautilus,* or the closest to it, at least.

My unblinking eyes clicked, rotating. I accelerated the portside propellers, following my charted course for the day, searching for metals to reclaim in areas not picked clean. Corporate, looking through my eyes, would be happy with my efficiency today. I was very good at finding what others missed.

Pretend, I told myself. *Just pretend and trust in luck.* The city plans and chaotic reports leading up to the last of the retreat from the waves served as my only guide. *Luck had saved my life, hadn't it?*

"*Go Undersea, Young Man. Help Reclaim Our Nation,*" the recruitment poster read the day my mother, coughing, brought me from the shantytown.

She half dragged me through the building's door, out of the oppressive heat. "Sign my boy up."

The recruiter smiled, half his teeth replaced with gold ones. "You want him as he is, or can we more or less fully upgrade him?" He poured a glass of water and grinned.

"What, uh, will full upgrading him mean?"

The fellow's eyes looked hard as he first appraised me. "Bigger bonus for you—if he's healthy and as young as he seems."

"He's ten…no, eleven, I think."

"You eleven, boy?"

I was eyeing the glass of water. "Yeah."

He nodded, offering a ghastly smile of gold capped teeth. "Here, boy, drink up." He took out a second glass, poured and raised it before my ma, then drew back. "He's real nice eyes," the recruit said. "Folks like that color, ma'am. Why don't you and I have a private chat about the rest and the different incentives?"

She nodded, and he handed her the glass of water, then poured me more. I drank it down, feeling drowsy. "We'll be right back, Rodney."

I blinked, finding it difficult to see. I never saw her again. If I had, I think I would have killed her.

These days, making the undrinkable, too-abundant waters of the Atlantic Ocean potable meant building desalination plants along the length of the coast. That required resources from the lost land, which literally lay beneath me.

A siren blared, and the computer said through my aural implants, *"Metallic objects detected two hundred meters dead ahead."*

"Sonar," I said aloud.

Ping.

An enhanced image formed in my mind.

"Reduce speed, drop anchors in five seconds," I ordered as Cap had done.

"Acknowledged."

The *Nautilus's* engines whined in reverse. The anchor jettisoned, dragged and snagged, while the floor beneath my feet lurched. "Probe."

A section of the habitat's gray shell irised and a camera, mounted on a multi-finned jet, shot forward. I steered its travel with my right-hand remote control.

The probe transmitted an image to my retina. The shape was unmistakable. There was the chassis of a twisted minivan blocking the cavern of what had been a parking garage.

"Set down the collection bay," I said, pretending to be the ever-productive tin man, knowing Corporate monitored my feeds.

I tried never to think too much about who might be looking through my eyes these days as I went about my duties. It didn't use to be this way. I still thought of myself as human, but that was before I became the last member of the *Nautilus's* crew.

Some things about my now being the only member of the ship's compliment I didn't mind. When we had a crew, I caught Pat, the most unlamented of my crewmates, drinking on duty and told him I would report his breech to the captain.

He glared at me. "You know, someone likely just wanted your old eyes because they were a lovely shade of green."

I seethed but offered a smile as the ever-pleasant cyborg.

Pat chuckled. "Probably the same person took your manhood for a joy toy."

I blanked, finding myself strangling him one-handed.

Cap slid down the ladder from the bridge. "Disengage, Rodney! Disengage!"

I stepped back, ever obedient, as Pat fell to the deck coughing and gasping.

"Wait for me in my cabin," Cap ordered.

"Aye, sir," I replied, turning, marching off.

Minutes later, he entered the cabin and secured the hatch. "Lad, do that again and I'll put you on report and lock out your feeds."

Leaving me in a living hell, deaf and blind.

"Look, Rodney, you're our tin man. This habitat depends on you more than any of us. Oh, we can pilot and crew this monstrosity, but you are its heart and soul. You can't afford to lose it like that, ever."

"He shouldn't have said that."

"I'm putting him on report for being drunk on duty. He's not going to enjoy the next week. And, believe me, no one on this crew will ever make a remark like that again."

They never did. I almost wished they could have.

"Nautilus, how you doing out there?"

I turned toward the sound unconsciously. The satellite feed going directly to the nerve of my left ear. "Control, approaching my designated target area."

"I need you to put that on hold."

I frowned. "I have a quota to make."

"Corporate's orders. We have some problems heading your way."

"Storm or pirates?"

"Neither. Corporate has a situation and the fact we still haven't a new crew to send out to you offers a valuable opportunity to evaluate it."

"Nautilus Six, here's the relevant download."

My eyes grew bright as the download speared through me like a sudden drop in temperature. Knowledge flooded me. You could turn back the evolutionary clock and give dolphins feet and chickens, well, rather sharp inwardly curved teeth, even scales instead of feathers. Genes occasionally mutated, re-activating old DNA. Corporate's Science Division decided in the name of circumstance and cost effectiveness to foster characteristics—very old characteristics.

"We need to know what is interfering with our operations."

"Understood, sir."

"They are on their way to your position now."

My connections followed the sonar tracks of my new crew members and the rather substantial object they towed behind their jets. My probe sent back an image of a twenty-foot cage of metallic links, which I recognized as one of the new style fisheries that the mobile habitats could tow. I heard a clang as they started mooring the fishery to the hull.

One of my new colleagues swam past the probe too fast for me to see her gills. But it was definitely a her. Corporate had not made any male mers.

Politicians still had constituents in the "Dry States," fearing damnation more than ever and dreading what corporations might do in the name of survival and profit. Having no mermen at least assured that the mermaids could never breed.

Such thinking was also why *Nautilus* was unarmed. After all, Corporate claimed we could depend on the Coast Guard to deal with any issues that might come up.

"Surface contact," I announced six months before, locked in position on the bridge.

Cap looked at the main screen. "Raise scope."

I sent a sensor to the surface, "Contact does not read as metallic, sir."

The image that appeared on the screen showed masts, sails, and an American flag. Cap sighed, "Coast Guard, with one old machine gun. How nice. We've a training cruise on that top-of-the-line cutter."

I focused on the sailors.

Cap shook his head. "Rodney, I don't envy that captain. Those farm boys clearly look seasick."

"Range increasing," I reported. "They are leaving our area."

"Doubt they even saw our float sensor. That old thing doubtless doesn't even have sonar." He looked away from the screen, sighing, "Maintain observation. Down sensor."

I fought back the memory.

Clang.

I focused on the task at hand, disengaged, and went to the hatch, cycling it at my signal. Through the observation glass in the inner airlock, I saw her sitting there, gasping, adapting to the environment as seawater receded into the floor drains.

The depictions of mermaids in fanciful old cartoons and movies accompanying the definition of "mermaid" did not compare to the real thing. She was hairless, her skin thicker and smooth like a dolphin or a manatee. She rose naked on her two legs, her feet and hands webbed.

She looked back at me through the glass and smiled. She had pearly white sharp teeth. As the pressure equalized, I signaled, allowing the hatch to cycle. There was a hiss of air. "Welcome aboard."

She looked at me.

I stood aside, making room for her to exit the lock.

She walked around me. When she spoke, it was as if breathing and talking at the same time were a matter of concentration, "Captain." She frowned. "You...have been...here...how long?"

"Four years. How long have you been a mermaid?"

"All...my...life," she replied, her facial expression difficult to read, but I would consider it tinged with humor for the moment. She glanced down at my pants. "You...fully...adapted?"

I chose not to reply.

Shaking her head, she said, "Sorry…unfair to…ask… Not…completely…used to…speaking…to others…out of water."

"You aren't fully adapted, either."

"No," she nodded.

"Corporate informed me of your needs. However, the cabins may not be suitable for you."

"Cabins? We…just…need space…to sleep."

"There are three cabins."

She nodded. "Two cabins…all…we need."

"They are five of you?"

She canted her head. "Yes… Five… Not all…come aboard…same time."

"Oh, joy."

"Not Joy… Choi."

My eye sockets swiveled.

"My name…is Choi."

"Rodney. Rodney Corey."

"Your designation is Tin Man, Nautilus Six," my watcher chided.

I ignored that, knowing sharing my name was a victory of sorts— even a pale one.

She came up to me, placing her hands on my cheeks, turned my head, "No…gills?"

"No, but even without my suit tank, I can hold my breath for rather long stretches. I also exhale less carbon dioxide than an unmodified human."

"Your…eyes?" she asked as the cameras irised, catching her reflection.

"See better than yours in water and without."

Nautilus, though fairly large, did not offer much in the way of amenities. Plants grew in the hydroponic overhangs, providing fruits and vegetables, adding to the air exchangers' efficiency.

Choi glanced around as she walked with me as Corporate watched through my mechanical eyes. "Access to crew quarters is either by these ladders or by vator. There is one cabin on this level, the Captain's quarters. It is now open to create the wardroom dining area next to the galley. Feel free to utilize it. I have no need. The cabins can also serve as escape pods in case of emergency."

She frowned.

"I guess that will not be an issue for you." I gestured. "Engineering is above the cargo bay. Crew cabins are forward of it, below the bridge. The main lift can take up to three people to the surface when we are not submerged. It is also decompression capable."

"No…need…of it."

"Uh, yes."

"Power?"

"We have a small nuclear power plant, converted from an old missile. It runs the Ripper, compactor, engines, and all the systems, particularly life support."

She canted her head.

"This…habitat…armed?"

"No," I replied. "We used to have a pistol in the weapons locker. No longer."

"Habitats…have…been…lost."

"Yes, but only to accidents," I replied, stating Corporate's official line, careful to not let a hint of bitterness show.

She looked around, winced, glancing at the lighting, which benefited the hydroponic greenery.

"I can shift the LEDs to a softer frequency."

"We…must be…concerned…about…vita-min D…deficiency too… Leave it…please."

I wondered about that, not wanting to think about the sections of my revealed skin across my upper torso, arms and legs that depended on that lighting to maintain my health as well. Choi's smooth, hairless skin was rather pearlescent. I was still human enough to notice much more, if not visibly react to it.

"We will…need to…moisten…our skin…at times."

"Each cabin offers a shower, both sonic and water." I gestured, feeds showing the one Pat and Engineer Martin had shared.

Rat-a-tat. *The engineer was flung backward as the men dressed in Corporate jackets fired their machine guns. Bullets laced out as Cap cried, "Pat, get back!" The rest were caught in the open on the barge's deck, preparing to lock on the bay to upload our haul. "Seal up!" Cap shouted.*

Pat screamed, turning to flee back toward the raised lift's hatch as I secured it, lowering it back into the hull. Pat cursed, toppling off the side into the sea as bullets laced across the hull to his right.

"Rod...ney?"

I turned my head and met her concerned gaze. "Sorry, I was focused on a diagnostic."

Shaking her head, she said, "You...alone...long...time?"

I hesitated. "I am never alone. The *Nautilus* keeps me company."

"Not good...to swim...alone."

So says the dolphin, I could not help but think.

"Show me...how...operate...shower."

I led her to the captain's cabin, keyed the retractable pallet on the right, the desk with an old-style keyboard on the left, recessing it above the storage lockers, one of which had a padlock.

"Captain's personal effects," I lied at her look of curiosity.

The screen built into the upper left wall offered a view of the floating fishery and her siblings stowing the jets. I pressed a panel. The wall swiveled, revealing the shower and head. She frowned, staring uncertainly at the head.

"How hot do you like the water?" I asked.

Her eyes blinked ever so slowly. Stepping into the three-sided unit, she replied, "Not...too...hot... Where's...soap?"

I reached over and tapped a tile on the wall. There was a click. I stared at the razor and shaving cream. Cap's toothbrush, container of toothpaste, a bar of soap and a plastic bottle of shampoo lay beside it.

She squeezed past me, turning the shower handle. "Soap...my...back?" she asked ever so innocently.

I backed away, knowing Corporate was as likely as surprised as I was. "I must return to overseeing the ship's systems."

I stood on the bridge, jacked into the ship's systems, trying to decide what to do. *Patience,* I told myself, watching Choi via the feeds Corporate monitored, then realized Corporate seemed distracted, intent only on views of the mermaids.

I signaled a remote in the workshop. The equipment activated. No one noticed.

I willed my heart rate not to rise, looping the feed and got to work, knowing I might only have minutes.

Choi soon came dripping out of the cabin. "I...should...bring...some of...my sisters...aboard."

"I would be happy to make dinner. My former crewmates considered me a good cook."

Smiling, Choi replied, "Only...if we...may...bring...an offering."

"I know just the thing."

Choi returned with her friends, who brought the main course. I made a salad harvesting the latest hydroponic offerings. They stared as I boiled a large pot of water. Choi frowned as she gave me the crabs. "What...are...you...doing?" she asked as I checked the pot.

I smiled. "My former captain once told me that this is what the Chesapeake Bay was known for. I figured you might like it."

They all canted their heads and frowned.

"Or would you prefer to eat some of the pastes Corporate provides? It has all the vitamin supplements a cyborg requires—or a human crew in an emergency. I guarantee it will taste awful to you, too."

They shrilled when I dropped the first crab into the boiling water. I clamped my hands over my ears, ordering my receptors to the lowest setting.

They hurried over and grabbed back their still living crabs, clutching them close. I lowered my hands and brought back up the sound. "We...like them...this way," Choi rasped.

"Uh, want some melted butter on them?"

They frowned.

Emotion welled as Choi and the others looked at the screens around the bridge like Cap and the crew used to. Clenching my fists at my sides, I could almost imagine the crew here instead.

Yet, the mermaids walking *Nautilus'* deck were disturbing. Perhaps the men of the other Corporate habitats and submersibles were similarly affected. Crews had their frictions and there were no females aboard, particularly naked ones even with thick, supple hide for skin.

Choi frowned, clearly not understanding the operating systems.

I could see Cap ordering the crew to stations.

"Rodney, report on the desalination units, the heat exchangers, and CO2 levels. Sonar, what do you have?"

Pat, wearing that damned baseball cap, answered from the bridge as we crisscrossed what once had been called Maryland and Delaware. "Cap, we've got the barge coming in."

"Confirmation code?"

"Received, sir," Pat replied.

"They're early," Cap said, then smiled. *"So, the beer will be on me tonight."*

I took a deep breath, pushing back the memory.

Choi glanced at me. "You…all…right?"

With my unblinking stare, I replied, "Fine." Oddly, that's when I also realized she smelled better than the regular crew, which I doubted Corporate monitoring would notice.

The *Nautilus* passed over another former thoroughfare, dragging the fishery behind it. We could not make great speed, but speed was not the point. I had chosen the salvage destination gleaned from clues from Social Media records.

The building still stood, rising from the water, the walls on the west side were caved in, and the upper floors were missing. Scavengers had been to this street before me, but that was all the better. They had made way for the *Nautilus* and what they had been searching for was not to be found in this particular building. Jewelry stores and the hope of finding treasure left in haste due to the rising waters, left behind the least valuable. They were anything but to me, in this thirsty and starving world.

Positioned over my target, I set the anchors. The Ripper soon snaked forward out of the front of the bay. An overturned dump truck blocked the way, which I considered part of the "waste not, want not" category.

I swam out of the lock in what was part wetsuit, part bodysub to verify the seals secured to the conveyor in the bay before beginning the harvesting sequence, which would convey the materials, compacting them for collection by a Corporate barge.

"Nautilus Six, you copy?" Control radioed, having to relay now that I was no longer linked through the submersible's system.

"Copy." I settled to the sea floor, crushing fragmented concrete rubble under my feet. Probes took position to watch the process from several angles. I saw through my feeds, the Ripper suck the vehicle towards its maw, its teeth beginning to spin. The truck vanished as the Ripper chewed it up.

"Fifteen credits value has been credited toward your monthly quota."

"Thank you," I replied automatically, ever the faithful tin man. The way now cleared, the Ripper slowed, stopped. "Good boy," I sent.

"Who are you talking to?" I suddenly heard through the water.

I turned my head as a mermaid swam over.

"Did you say that?" I sent.

Eyes fixed on me, Choi nodded, bubbles burst from her mouth as I heard, *"Yes."*

"Care to help?"

She looked at the cavern, which in a former day would have been the entry to a pawn shop. *"What do you seek?"*

I directed a sonar sweep inside. "Treasure."

Choi canted her head, then swam ahead.

"How do you find the new household arrangements?" Control's psychologist asked.

"You see and hear everything I do."

Choi looked into the safe I had ripped out of the floor, missed by the looters and later scavengers. The door laying twisted feet away. She frowned, shook her head, finding only papers and once valuable cash.

"But how do you feel about it?" my watcher asked.

"It is good having help again."

"Just that?"

"Efficiency was what I was created for." *Though I know that was a lie, it was the Corporate creed.*

Choi peered into the safe, reached in and clawed the insides. *'Ah.'* She pried open a hidden compartment in the back. The less legal wares revealed. She passed me a handful of diamond and ruby rings, which I held up to my eyes, then a gold pocket watch, then reached in again, drawing out a jeweled necklace, holding it up to her neck.

"It's you, my dear."

She clicked, which I realized meant she was laughing.

After looking at each piece, I placed our haul in a transport bag.

"Estimated value, eighty-six thousand eight hundred dollars, credited to your monthly quota. Congratulations, you have exceeded your quota for the month."

And then some. "Time to go."

She swam past.

"Tin Man, your vital signs are spiking."

"I am looking forward to the oiling I can now afford."

"You are not attracted to the mermaid?"

"Attracted? I'm a cyborg."

"We have noted unusual behavior in the crews they work with."

"Unusual how?"

"Higher levels of aggression among submariners than expected."

"Likely their crews needed liberty."

"Perhaps…"

A different voice, *'Nautilus Six, a barge will reach your position tomorrow and collect your quota. The mermaids' catch will be collected in three days."*

The psychologist added, *"You will report any unusual activity on their part."*

"Acknowledged."

The next day, we anchored over what had been the Potomac. The barge in the distance appeared on sonar. They provided the Corporate recognition signal. I went out through the lock, deactivating the Ripper, putting it in conveyer mode.

A mermaid swam frantically toward me and sirened. My ears felt like they would shatter as my feeds went down.

A moment later I realized it was Choi in front of me, pulling me back as a wooden log headed toward the *Nautilus Six* faster than the current. A mermaid swam away from it, which puzzled me before it struck.

There was an explosion, and my feeds went down as bubbles roiled around us.

Cap fell to the rat-a-ta-tat of machine gun fire and rasped over our link, "It's a trap."

His right side bleeding from the bullets that had ripped into him, Cap gasped, "Get clear."

I summoned the lift to retract at max, cut the anchors loose, and followed Cap's private pre-existing orders. I always surreptitiously over-pressurized the bay transfer shaft. The first load of scrap metals within suddenly spewed forth at pressures the designers never intended. The thieves knew the habitat was unarmed, but it, like me, was never truly.

I heard their screams through Cap's commlink and sent the Nautilus *backing away.*

I woke with a start or, perhaps, I should say, a re-start. My eyes came back online, then my ears. *"Nautilus Six, do you copy?"* Control shouted. *"Nautilus Six, do you copy?"*

I sat up in the airlock. *"Nautilus, here."*

"Nautilus Six, do you copy?"

"Rod...ney?" Choi said, leaning rather close.

"Nautilus Six, do you copy? If you can hear me, the barge missed their check-in. Suspect the barge is no longer in friendly hands. They should be on your position in approximately ten minutes. Six, do you copy?"

"Computer, diagnostic," I ordered.

"Damage to snorkel sustained," the computer replied. *"Transmission relays damaged."* Minor damage alerts now fed to my connections.

My hand twitched as Choi brushed up against my arm, reaching over to place her webbed fingers around my face, looking deep into my mechanical eyes. "They can't see or hear us now, Choi. Was that your plan?"

She canted her head. "Plan?"

181

"The barge is not in Corporate's hands. We do not have time to play games. You do not trust them and Corporate does not trust you. Out with it."

Those too-wide eyes stared at me. "Don't...like them."

"You do not have to—or do you think I would choose this?" I said, raising my hands with their retracted leads to grip her wrists.

She lowered her head. "We...not like...them...watching."

"Sorry. What I see, they see."

"You...seeing...doesn't...make us...feel...dirty."

"You damaged the snorkel antenna."

"They...don't...know that."

"I guess that should go in the log, as will the fact that we do not have time to make repairs."

Smiling, she asked, "What...are...you...planning?"

"Have you raised the anchors?"

"No... Haven't...learned...to...drive yet."

"Right," I replied, not believing that for an instant.

"Do you...have...any...weaponry?"

I frowned, releasing my grip on her wrists. "This vessel is unarmed."

"Is it...really?"

"I multitask."

"What...weaponry?"

Shrugging, I said, "I may have whipped up a little something."

She grinned, showing those wicked teeth. "Heard...what...you... did...to pirates."

"Oh, you mean the accident... The malfunction."

She nodded. "Good...man."

"No, I am a monster," I replied, and meant it.

The barge slowed as the tug propelling it reversed engines.

"Nautilus Six, permission to come aboard. We understand you are short-handed."

I acknowledged their message by simply raising the lift toward the surface, which also signaled Choi and the other mermaids. What can

I say? A cyborg's eyes may spy for Corporate, but that doesn't mean they owned my soul.

I had access to Corporate's network and all its unrestricted knowledge. After all, knowledge of the old world was necessary to making a profit. How dangerous could knowing how to build primitive explosive devices out of common household items really be?

The lift bobbed to the surface as the sun's glare was at its worst. A crew member leaped from the deck onto it and tied off a mooring line. A ball cap concealed his face as he gestured for another member of the crew to board. He backed toward the airlock as he worked with the mooring lines.

I ordered the lift to rise. After all, we were one big happy family. Then again, turnabout was fair play. My probes showed a mermaid reaching the barge's hull, locking the first of the homemade limpet mines to it, her sister doing the same shortly thereafter.

The sailor suddenly turned, flipped the access pad and keyed the lock to the hatch, which cycled open as he drew a pistol and smiled up at the camera. "Hey, Rodney."

"Pat," I gasped, then as the last mermaid swam clear, I secured the lift, trapping him, and set off the charges.

The explosions tore into the barge's fuel tank. The concussive waves rocked the *Nautilus* and my unwelcome guest, who fell to his knees.

"Welcome back, Crewman."

He groaned. "Asshole, what did you do?"

"I suggest you tell me what happened to the barge's crew."

"Go to hell."

"So, they are all dead."

He began to sweat. "Not all of them. Anything happens to me and they die."

"For the record, heart rate and respiration indicate you are lying. He stands here as a pirate and mutineer."

The computer replied, *"Acknowledged."*

"Carry out sentence in three, two, one."

"Pressurizing."

Pat screamed and made quite a mess of the lift.

Choi swam by one of my feeds, looking sad. I thought, *It's not like we needed the lift.*

Five mermaids were assigned to *Nautilus,* but a sixth I had never met came aboard, which explained exactly why they were less than trusting of Corporate. She was rather pregnant.

"Rod...ney... What...you...did..." Choi said as her friends stared.

"I won't tell you I'm sorry. He murdered my friends, and if given a chance, he would have killed me and stolen this vessel."

"Corporate...will not...understand."

"They will decide that I'm malfunctioning and too unstable to leave online."

"They...not...leave...our sister...live, either."

"No. They cannot. What is it you want?"

"Need...*Nautilus*... Need you."

"Me?"

"Big...strong...man."

"I'm not a man. I'm a—"

"Not monster... We not...monsters."

They looked at me, smiling.

"So, you want this ship to become what? A nursery?"

Choi made a sound that sounded like laughter.

"What's so funny?"

Choi came over and hugged me. "You...make...good father."

"What?"

'*Nautilus Six! We are tracking you by satellite heading out to sea. Do you copy? Six, do you copy? Rodney, if you hear me, all the mermaids have abandoned their posts. Repeat, the mermaids working the coast have abandoned their posts and are heading toward the Chesapeake Bay. Report immediately!* Nautilus Six! *Damn it, can you hear me?*"

I silenced the feed. Choi and I were rather busy. While four mermaids were manning the bridge, her formerly rather shy sister was writhing in the airlock, which was half filled with seawater.

"Push," Choi urged, the jeweled necklace about her throat catching the light.

The baby abruptly swam free, not breathing, although her eyes were wide open and taking in the world. The gills on her neck did not flutter. I cut the cord as Choi encouraged the infant to breathe, which is when her gills fluted.

"She has red hair," I noted in surprise.

"Yes... Beautiful...is it...not?"

"But you don't have hair."

"We...do...as...children."

"Oh."

The new mother slipped beneath the recycling water, hugging her baby close.

I grinned. "A real little mermaid."

Choi nodded. "But no...mer...men."

"Sorry, no men here, either."

Choi leaned close, kissing me. "So...wrong... You...much...better."

About the Author

D.H. Aire is the author of over twenty science fiction and fantasy novels. They include his epic fantasy Highmage's Plight and Hands of the Highmage Series, and more recently those of the Knights Tower and the satiric adventure of surviving the Bigfoot apocalypse in his Apocalypse Knot Series, whose third book, *Bigfoot and the Four Horsemen* will be published in 2025.

"Tin Man" is Aire's third story to appear in an Enrapturing Tales anthology.

He resides in the Washington DC metropolitan area and is a member of SFWA. You can learn more by visiting his website at DHAire.net. You can follow him at Dare 2 Believe on Facebook and on X, formerly Twitter, @DHAire15.

Unnatural Waters

by

Paul Lonardo

Unnatural Waters

The six retired Rhode Island State Police detectives at the Westerly Nursing Home for Men agreed that the most savage and cunning of murders are committed within the sanctity of marriage. Each man wagered twenty dollars, with the pot going to the man who told the most intriguing story involving a case they investigated in which a spouse got away with murder.

The sitting room in which the men gathered was spacious and functional. Most of the other rooms in the private facility were equally expansive, but to these former troopers, the nursing home remained nothing more than a glorified prison. Despite the Georgian architecture, magnificent seaside location, friendly attendants, and other amenities, they were prisoners of their deteriorating bodies.

The room would have been entirely in darkness if not for the stealthy glow of pipe tobacco embers and the blue light from the twenty-gallon glass aquarium by the door.

Rebecca, the nurse practitioner and the facility's chief administrator, strictly forbid their little after-hours gathering, so the men spoke in hushed tones. While each of the other men spun some time-bloated tale of their bygone gumshoe days, pensioned-off Captain Richard Cahill just sat back and waited for his turn, knowing that none could be more diabolical than the murder account that he was about to relate.

Only Samuel Hawes remained silent. While he had recovered physically from the stroke he'd suffered several years earlier, his mental faculties continued to slowly erode.

"Congressman Deavers would have preferred being killed by any of the methods you good men just mentioned instead of the way his life ended," Cahill said when the others had finished. He combed his smoky gray mustache with his fingers. His face was bullish, almost unsightly, but his jowls were taut, and he was the only one in the room who boasted a full head of hair.

"Are you alluding that Congressman Deavers didn't die by his own hand?" Brian Marion spoke loudly from outside the circle of men, where he sat to avoid the second-hand pipe smoke that "Buzzy" Tomasso and Sid Katz were producing in thick plumes.

"Will you keep it down, you old piker," Buzzy said in an exasperated whisper. "Do you want Rebecca to hear us? Either join us in the circle or adjust your hearing aid, but keep your whiny voice down." Concluded, he deliberately blew a contrail of smoke in Marion's direction.

"There is no allusion about it," Cahill clarified. "His wife arranged his murder."

"Elizabeth?" Harlan Phahler scoffed. "I don't believe it."

"The press would have had a field day if there was the least bit of suspicion leveled against her," Marion stated. "You headed that investigation. Why was there no mention of her involvement in your report?"

"After what I saw that night on the jetty out behind the Deavers estate in Newport, I swore for the sake of my own sanity that I'd never tell a living soul about it," Cahill explained. "Besides, if I spoke one word about it, they would have put me into a place exactly like this one, only with padded walls. So, suicide the report reads, and suicide it will stay. But I don't have to convince any of you that a man does not kill himself by pulling out his insides and having them spill out onto the floor *and then* slit his own throat. Puzzling enough was why a powerful man like Deavers, a respected attorney and politician, and likely future governor, would choose to end his own life."

"I don't believe it," Phahler said again. The 80-year-old ex-police chief was a tall man, though scoliosis severely bowed his spine. "There's nothing you say that will convince me otherwise. Elizabeth Deavers was surely not a woman capable of such treachery, even if her husband's perpetual philandering might have warranted it. Such a lovely, refined woman. Impossible, I say."

"I never said she was the murderer," Cahill exclaimed. "I said she arranged it."

"She hired a hit man?" Buzzy put forth.

"Not exactly. It was no man."

The all-too-obvious solution to this riddle hung in the air for a moment. No one spoke until Cahill dismissed what everyone was thinking. "Nor woman, either."

Cahill was amused by the reaction of the other men. Their wrinkled faces cloaked their expressions of puzzlement. Samuel Hawes, while listening intently, raised to his lips a leather-bound hip flask that his son had smuggled in on his last visit. After taking a sip, he held it out, offering to share the brandy with the others, but there were no takers.

"What exactly did you see that night?" Sid Katz was speaking for everyone. As usual, his words were few, but carefully chosen and explicit. Precision marked the man like feathers on a duck.

"First, let me explain a few things about Elizabeth Deavers," Cahill began. "I agree with Lieutenant Phahler. This was a woman beyond reproach. She was someone who took her marriage vows very seriously. She proved that time and time again, standing by her husband through each subsequent affair, sordid as they may have been. For Elizabeth Deavers, her marriage ended the only way she believed one ever should: in death."

Cahill let his prefatory comments percolate a while before he continued. "That said, the moment I viewed her husband's remains, I knew it was no simple suicide, even though it was apparent that the *coup de grâce* was the throat wound, which was, indeed, self-inflicted. The fact was, he had damn near decapitated himself in the process. Shockingly, the disembowelment came before. And I might add, the means by which this mutilation had occurred could not be determined with any certainty. It looked to me like his abdomen had split open by itself."

"How aggressively did you interrogate Elizabeth?" Buzzy inquired around a mouth full of pipe smoke. "She clearly had a motive."

"Doubtless, there would be myriad suspects," Sid Katz said. "Any number of scornful boyfriends and vengeful husbands, even overprotective brothers or fathers, may have been driven to commit such a crime of passion or retribution."

"Like all of you, I never suspected Elizabeth. I didn't know who did it, and to be honest, I didn't care. Truth be told, I was far from enthusiastic about finding the perpetrator. Had I discovered a man responsible, I may have been tempted to shake the bastard's hand. Jonathon Deavers was a complete and total slimeball, but it was still my job to see that justice was served, even for someone so deplorable."

"It just doesn't make sense," Marion muttered from behind the group of men. "With such a grievous injury as you described to his abdomen, why would Deavers slit his own throat?"

"I'm getting to that. Bear with me." Cahill sat back, observing each of the captivated men. "As you all know, Elizabeth Deavers was born into wealth and spent much of her time in philanthropic pursuits. She was very active in the community, involving herself with numerous charities. Not being able to have children herself, she gave back to others in many ways. She also worked as a researcher at the Newport Oceanographic Institute. At the time of her husband's demise, she was away on some expedition at sea, so her alibi was rock solid. Thus, if it is hard evidence of guilt you require, I can only provide circumstance. What I do know is that if you had been at the murder scene, your own professional instincts would have told you that the whole thing smacked of something sinister, like something unnatural had taken place there."

"I never knew you to have such a flare for the dramatic, Captain," said Buzzy with a wry grin.

"I also thought myself immune to such theater," Cahill conceded. "This was the one time, and as you know, I retired immediately after the medical examiner confirmed my conclusion that the death of Jonathon Deavers was a result of suicide."

There was a sudden noise upstairs. The men all started and looked up, half expecting to see Rebecca come fluttering down the stairs in her purple robe that was missing its top button. That sight would have been preceded the sound of her fuzzy gorilla feet slippers dragging across the rug on the landing as she made her way to the study to harangue them about the facility's policy forbidding unsupervised assemblies after hours. But no such sound came, and after several uncertain moments, Cahill proceeded.

"As you all probably would have guessed, Jonathan Deavers was not alone the night he was killed," Cahill continued. "In Deavers' kitchen bin that night, I discovered an empty wine bottle and a tray of partially eaten caviar. On the kitchen counter were two used long-stem wine glasses, which *were* dusted for prints, evidence that I later chose to destroy. I'll tell you why momentarily. However, there were also indications that Deavers was not expecting company that night, judging by his attire and the condition of his study, where legal briefs from a case he was working on were spread across his desk. I must also note that only the basement door leading directly out to the beach was unlocked, so it was likely that the uninvited caller appeared from that location upon entering, and later exiting, the estate."

"I fail to see the significance the visitor's means of entry would have on the case, Richard," Marion said. "Or are you set on diverting us?"

"I am relating the facts as they were revealed to me, and I will allow each of you to come to your own conclusions. If I am crazy, let the sane man among you condemn me." Cahill settled back in his chair and twirled one corner of his mustache with the index finger and thumb of his right hand. "But remember, these are the facts and should not be overlooked, no matter how trivial."

"Touché," Sid Katz said. "Go on, Captain."

Cahill adjusted himself in the stiff wing chair once again. When he was comfortable, he focused his gaze out the wide picture window as if it reflected the past. "Deavers' study contained thousands of volumes," he explained. "One unusual volume had been removed from the shelves. A medical journal. It was prominently laid out on the desk atop his work papers, open to an entry under OBSTETRICS."

"Had a pregnant concubine showed up at his door claiming he was the father?" Marion offered.

Cahill slowly shook his head.

"He found out that his wife was pregnant, but he was not the father," Marion began, changing directions. "What a turn of fate! Deavers couldn't bear to live with that knowledge, and he did himself in."

Cahill never stopped shaking his head as he listened to Marion's explanations. In the silence that followed, he plucked at the whiskers above his lip. He knew he had all of them in the palm of his hands. "While Elizabeth wasn't due back from her three-week excursion at sea for several days yet," he began, "that night Deavers made a frantic call to a doctor friend, arranging to be seen first thing the next morning. He was very vague about the purpose of the visit, but he made it clear to Dr. Schuler that it was an emergency. He never made it to the appointment."

Marion spoke up with forced confidence. "Is it not obvious to all of you by now that Mrs. Deavers laced her husband's food or drink with some kind of drug or poison that rendered him mad, causing him to mutilate himself?"

Cahill gave no acknowledgement to this supposition but continued with his chronicle. "I must admit to you that the horrifying truth did not occur to me right away, even after a thorough investigation. Then I saw the thing for myself."

"For the love of Pete, Cahill," Buzzy snapped, "Stop speaking in tongues and give us the low-down already. How did Elizabeth Deavers conspire in the death of her husband?"

"After the funeral, I went to see Elizabeth at the Newport beach home, to ask her a few follow-up questions. I spotted her outside on the farthest point of a jetty, which extended nearly a hundred yards into the ocean. It was overcast and drizzling. As I plodded carefully across the slick rocks, I called her name, but she couldn't hear me over the pounding surf. Her back was to me, and she was staring out at the raging sea. The water was rough, the spray obscuring her already shadowy form. I finally reached her, and I was standing just a few feet away when I screamed her name and asked her if I might have a word with her. She half-turned and I saw she was cradling a tightly swathed bundle in her arms."

"I knew it," Marion said much too loudly, before lowering his voice considerably when he noticed the disapproving stares of the other men. "She *had* been pregnant. She had gone off somewhere to have the child because it had been sired to her by a lover, who then murdered Deavers."

"Afraid not," Cahill said with satisfaction as the other man's smile dissolved. "After apologizing for my bluntness, I told Elizabeth that I believed she knew who her husband had been with the night he was killed, and that the only hope we had of solving the murder was talking with the last person who had seen him alive."

"That's laying it on the line," said Sid Katz as he relit his pipe with a gold-leafed Zippo.

Cahill groomed his mustache, his eyes distant and reflective. "She just turned away from me, looking out to sea. When she didn't respond, I began thinking of ways to rephrase my question, to better reflect the urgency of the situation. When she finally spoke, I could barely hear her over the sound of the waves breaking on the jetty, and I wasn't sure I heard her right, but what she told me was not only odd, but incomprehensible to me. At least at the time."

"What did she say?" Phahler asked impatiently.

"She told me that humans are not the only species that mate for pleasure."

The men looked around at each other. Phahler had a cockeyed grin on his face.

"I, too, was taken aback by her remark," Cahill acknowledged. "She went on to tell me that what she found most interesting to study were sea creatures that are truly 'monoecious.' That is, having both male and female reproductive organs, and reproducing can reproduce asexually."

"You mean they screw themselves," Buzzy contributed. "That would make Marion monoecious."

Controlled laughter rippled through the ranks. A smile even played in the corners of Cahill's mouth for a brief moment. Marion, his cheeks coloring, glowered scornfully at his pipe-smoking antagonist.

"In such a genus, Elizabeth told me, there is no need for sex," Cahill continued, countenancing genuine unease, which suppressed any further laughter at Marion's expense. "Now, it could have been a shadow, but I thought I saw her mouth curl up into a sinister smirk, which never left her face as she explained how, in certain species of fish and amphibians, they can change from one sex to another. These animals produce sperm at one stage of their lives and eggs at another. She called it 'sequential hermaphroditism.' It was at that moment that she looked me full in the face. I saw her eyes, the color of cold slate, and in deadly seriousness she asked me what I thought would happen to the human race if its reproduction were to become asexual and men had to give birth."

"However did you respond to that?" Phahler asked.

"Before I could say anything, she focused her eyes back on the choppy surf and then told me about a previous voyage that she had taken with Newport Oceanographic Institute, to a coral reef off the Albanian coast in the Adriatic. She made inferences to reported sightings of mysterious creatures of alluring beauty that had been reported there."

There was an audible gasp among some men in the room.

"Now, I had been aware of the hyped-up stories that had been popping up in the news at that time about mermaids, or some such silliness, being spotted all around the world, including off the New England coast. Mind you, I'd never given credence to whimsy of any kind previously. Those of you who know me can vouch for that."

"Are you insinuating that she had been out looking for mermaids?" Buzzy asked incredulously.

"She told me she oversaw the Institute's most recent expedition in the North Atlantic, from which she had just returned. She said they had been exploring an atoll just east of Chappaquiddick that allegedly had been witness to similar sightings, described by fishermen as sea nymphs."

"Sea nymph," Phahler repeated. "My second wife was a sea nymph. I once came home to find her in bed with three sailors." He laughed alone, without humor. All eyes remained on Cahill.

"Did Mrs. Deavers ever find one?" Marion inquired.

"I asked Elizabeth the same question," Cahill told him. "She sighed, and with a tear in her eye, or maybe it was brine, she said she supposed that the mermaid legend was just that; a legend, conjures of lonely fishermen. I don't know what made me ask the question I did next. Perhaps it was an attempt to break the chilling silence between us, or maybe it was to stifle the cryptic chatter of the sea. Whatever the actual prompt, before I could appeal to my better judgment, I asked her if the methods of reproduction she described as occurring in fish could occur in mammals."

A light switched on upstairs in the Westerly Nursing Home for Men and the sound of someone stirring incited uneasiness among the men.

"What did she say?" Phahler demanded, not caring about the volume of his voice.

"She gave no response, but she looked at me with such a disturbing cast to her eyes that I almost turned away from her at once. I must admit, never has another person's stare held such a humbling sway over me. That's when the bundle in her arms shifted. I smiled and hooked a finger into the tangle of cloth. I was about to inquire about the child, but as the first syllable formed on my lips, the wrappings fell away. Every thought I had in my head broke off at once, and I shrank back in horror at the abominable infant. I almost slipped on the slick rocks underfoot as I recoiled."

"The child was deformed?" Marion probed.

Cahill's face soured with his recounting of the image. "Its mouth was a gaping, jawless maw, rife with needle-sharp teeth. The creature's flesh was translucent and coated with a clear, gummy substance. It possessed a single nostril, its eyes black chips of onyx. It was making a tiny suckling sound, as if it wanted to be nursed. And a rasping, gray tongue darted in and out of the buccal funnel that was its face."

"Good God!" Samuel Hawes rasped. Even in the room's dimness, Cahill could see a sickish green pallor imbue his face, appearing as if he might sick up the dinner he ate six hours earlier.

"Elizabeth seemed to hold back a laugh," Cahill continued as another light came on, illuminating the stairs behind them. Nobody looked up. "That did it for me. One of us was mad. It made no difference. Insanity loves company. I turned heel, anxious to be away from the urgent suckling sounds of this obscenity and the grinning face of the woman holding it in her arms.

"I looked back briefly as I jumped down off the rocks onto the beach. Elizabeth was almost out of sight, but she appeared to lean over and release the creature into the ocean, accompanied by a barely audible splash. I turned and left, never speaking to Elizabeth Deavers again, and never did I make mention to anyone what transpired on the jetty that afternoon until this very moment. I determined Jonathon Deavers' death to be a suicide and closed the book on the case."

Cahill took a deep breath and closed his eyes. When he opened them a moment later, he seemed to have gathered his thoughts and returned from that time and place in his past to focus on the men in the room once more.

"Are we to derive from all this that Elizabeth Deavers arranged an unnatural congress between her husband and some kind of mythical creature?" Phahler's tone was challenging.

"So, it was Congressman Deavers who was pregnant," Sid Katz concluded.

"Preposterous," shouted Marion.

"The congressman's tumescent belly must have been churning with the lifeform at the time he removed the volume on the subject of pregnancy and childbirth from his personal library," Buzzy deduced. "That's why he called his doctor. The rapidly growing embryo, seeking egress, finally burst from his stomach, and in desperate terror and agony, the congressman slit his own throat," he remarked with finality.

"Completely unfathomable." Marion insisted as soft footsteps descended the carpeted stairs.

"One thing I think we can all agree on is that the captain's story takes the prize," Sid Katz said, reaching into his wallet and removing a twenty-dollar bill.

"Pay up, men," Cahill instructed with a hearty laugh.

The money changed hands quickly.

"But what was the damning evidence you spoke of destroying?" Phahler wanted to know.

"The following day I heard from the crime lab," Cahill began, speaking quickly, "and I was informed that no fibers or prints other than those identified as belonging to Jonathan Deavers were found at the scene. However, a substance that was truly confounding was detected on the wine glasses, something that was described as '*an abundance of microscopic squamulose.*'"

None of the men took the bait. Cahill looked directly at Marion and said, "Fish scales."

"Up to your old tricks again, I see." Rebecca stood in the doorway with her hands on her hips. "Men and their fish stories." Her face was covered with a drying, green mud mask that flaked off as she spoke. Her hair was rolled in pink curlers, and she was wearing the purple robe with a missing button. The array of colors made her look like a macaw, or some other unusual bird. "You gentlemen know the rules do not allow for gatherings at this hour. And Mr. Hawes, I know you are aware that alcohol is strictly prohibited."

"Ah, it's just a little nip," Hawes said meekly in his defense.

"Come on then, let's go," Rebecca instructed. "Back to your rooms."

The men groaned as they got up out of their chairs and were escorted to the stairs. Rebecca was last to leave the room, and before walking out, she paused and glanced at the rectangular aquarium by the door. Among the exotic fish inside the tank were a coral reef decoration and a ceramic sunken ship. There was also a tiny mermaid ornament, and, clinging to the glass next to it, was the oddest-looking fish. It was long and tubular, attached to the glass by its mouth, which held several circular rows of tiny teeth. She heard it making a faint suckling sound as a gray tongue licked the algae off the inside of the glass.

Disgusting, Rebecca thought, wondering how she'd never noticed this tiny creature in the tank before. A shiver went up her spine as she left the sitting room, closing the door behind her.

About the Author

Paul Lonardo is a freelance writer and author with numerous titles, both fiction and nonfiction books. Paul has placed short stories and nonfiction pieces in various genre magazines and ezines. He is a contributing writer for several publications, including *Tales from the Moonlit Path*, and an HWA member. His latest anthology, *Dark Little Things*, features 25 short tales of dark fantasy and horror. Visit Paul's author website: www.thegoblinpitcher.com, and on Instagram @PaulLonardo13, and X: @PaulLonardo

Cinnamon and Sweat

by

Thea Hutcheson

Cinnamon and Sweat

man flailed in the water, the sinking ship behind him backlit by Apollo's chariot as the sun god headed for his stately home ahead of black clouds. The ship's painted sail disappeared into the depths of Poseidon's realm. The sea god would gladly take this latest tribute.

The storm had arrived as the ship, filled with soldiers and workers, approached the shore. Stupid to sail in the winter months and worse, not to anchor in some protected inlet long before Apollo rode down to his palace, but mortals, for all their brilliance, were often stupid or simply terrible gamblers.

Rain sleeted down; the steady hissing nearly drowned out the cries of the mortals below the high promontory overlooking the water near where King Aegeus leapt into the sea when he saw the black sails of his Theseus's ships.

Opis swam toward the man in her mortal shape, through water usually brilliant blue but now dark and frothy like the foam that Aphrodite rose from. Opis's father, Nereus, was always willing to help the hapless at sea and he commanded his daughters to do the same. Opis and her sisters cared about what went on in the clear blue sea off Greece's coast, so they did the work gladly.

Opis had rescued several passengers already, and she was growing tired. But one more. Surely, she could rescue one more. Diving under the waves, she came up behind the man, careful to avoid his flailing arms as she rescued him, pulling him by his long, curly, dark hair.

He struggled and Opis crooned to him, first in the language of the sea, and then, seeing that it made him frantic, in his own mother tongue. "Be still," she said. "I will pull you from the sea. I will return you to Gaia's breast. Be still."

He eyed her for a long moment, then nodded wearily.

She swam strongly through the thrashing waves, pulling him behind her, the rain pelting her skin. Inhaling, the smell of the storm mixed with the salt of the sea and, oddly, a hint of cinnamon suffused her. The combination gave her a sense of the vividness of life amid the tempest.

She kicked with her legs, wishing she had her tail as she made her way to the rocky shoreline. Once there, she clambered ashore and settled him in her arms, covering him as much as she could to protect him from the sleeting drops as he shivered, too weak yet to stand and make his way onto the land.

His arms were well-muscled, hewn by swinging the sword that still hung at his side, the angles of his face pleasing. He smelled of something…that same cinnamon, now combined with rank sweat.

Opis stroked his hair back away from his face, brushed the water from his curly beard. He was a man in his prime and her heart stirred with more than her usual affection for living beings.

At last, he pulled away from her arms and stood shakily. He took in her sleek body, her dark hair in this aspect threaded with pearls and bits of mother-of-pearl.

She blushed at his appreciation.

"My thanks, my lady, for you rescuing me. Hermes was coming for me and I despaired of crossing the River Styx with no one to leave a coin for my passage."

"You are welcome, good sir. But only tell me your name."

"Hebrides, gracious lady."

"Well, Hebrides, I am Opis."

"Fair Opis, you have my gratitude for saving me. You must be one of Nereus's daughters to have been in that raging storm."

"I am one of his fifty daughters," she said, lowering her gaze modestly.

"Then I swear on Poseidon's mighty trident that I shall make a sacrifice in your name before the next full moon," he said.

The air did not shimmer when the oath went out into the world as it did when gods declared their will.

"But now I must find my commander or someone to report to. And tell them I lost my shield and," he groped at his waist. "And all my wealth."

The rain sleeted down, but Opis had eyes made to see through the watery depths. She pointed out the path. "Follow it around the face of the promontory. The priests and soldiers have a village there."

"Again, my thanks, great lady."

"I am not great," Opis said, the darkness hiding her blush. "Only a younger daughter of Nereus, but I accept your thanks. I hope to see you again," she said, suddenly brave before this handsome soldier she had rescued from Poseidon's realm.

He smiled at her in a way that took her breath away with him when he made his way among the rocks up to the trail and disappeared into the darkness. She heard his sandaled feet slapping on the sodden path and listened until she heard them no more.

How handsome he is. How polite. And he offered to sacrifice to me!

Opis was not important like Thetis, mother of Achilles, or Amphitrite, Poseidon's own wife. Perhaps she could gain a reputation as a savior of mortals. Perhaps they would worship her and offer sacrifices to her on a dedicated altar. What would it be like to accept a sacrifice made only to her?

She slipped away from the rocky beach and back into the sea, returning to her water aspect, a mortal upper half and face with a curved tail below that ended in wide, diaphanous flukes. The entirety of her body covered with iridescent scales that flashed in the least light.

Never had her work caring for sailors and the creatures of the sea been so pleasurable. She would search for Hebrides's shield and his pouch. And whatever she found, she would tell him to offer back some portion to Poseidon, perhaps gaining some favor for himself.

She flipped her powerful tail and dove deep beneath the waves, searching for this newfound opportunity to please this mortal who made her heart beat so hard and fast. The cool water burned against the warmth of her cheeks.

Opis had been living for the last few months along the coast, watching the mortals build the grand new temple of marble to Poseidon. Perched on the high promontory overlooking the sea, the white marble shone like a beacon.

The mortals were always so busy, so involved in their work, so clever with their hands. Opis thought the temple, with its tall, stately columns and wide processional walkway winding up to the mount, would be as beautiful as the sea god's palace under the sea.

She watched the village and the craftsmen, looking for Hebrides. She had found three shields and four pouches with amber and nuggets of silver and two rings in them. Perhaps one of these would be his.

There! He walked down the path, even more handsome by daylight. His curly hair was pulled back from his face by a thong and boiled down his back in a black froth. She watched his steps, coiled with power. The sunlight burnished the muscles beneath his olive skin.

Opis waited, floating on the sea until he reached the bottom of the trail, then changed into her mortal aspect, and called to him.

He glanced around and she had to call twice more before he looked toward the water, where she lazily tread the water just off the rocks.

"My lady, you are my savior, are you not?"

Opis blushed. "I am. I have searched for your pouch and your shield. Perhaps one of these is yours?" She dragged them out of the water and brought them up onto the shore.

He joined her and inspected the shield. "This one is Keftian. See the double rounds top and bottom?" He lifted another. "This is a Dorian's *aspis.*" He set it down to hold up a bowled plate, the wood waterlogged, the bronze corroded by the salt water. "This is a *thyreos.*" He slipped the oval shield over his forearm. "Who knew Poseidon claimed so many?"

She smiled at his wonder. Who knew so much about shields?

He must be very smart. Smart and handsome.

"Poseidon rightfully claims everything that slips into his realm."

He set them back down. "Mine is like the *aspis* but has a bronze lion boss in the center. It has a dent on the left side where a Libyan tried to run me through with his lance."

His eyes gleamed as he inspected the pouches, hefting the silver and rubbing the amber. "None of these are mine, but I will take them to the village to see if anyone can claim them. I thank you, Lady Opas." He gathered the bags and stood. "I must be about my business now before my captain misses me."

"I will keep looking for you, but you must offer anything unclaimed to Poseidon, so he receives his own back," Opis said, ignoring that he mispronounced her name.

"Yes, please do keep looking."

"I shall see you before the full moon, then," she said.

"The full moon? Ah, yes. It should be very pretty from Poseidon's temple. Hopefully, the *Anemoi* will keep their winds to themselves so the clouds will not cover her lovely face."

Opis nodded eagerly. The moon was beautiful here, especially when her full face gazed down at the water. "Your sacrifice should be especially nice then."

Hebrides stared at her for a long moment, then nodded. "Yes, very beautiful. I must go." He scooped up the bags, bowed his head in deference, and headed back up the trail.

Why did he go back up the path when he had been headed down? Ah, yes, to see who owned the pouches.

Opis returned the shields to the water and scoured the sea bottom for other pouches and shields. She brought up his shield and he was very grateful, which made her heart sing. She told him to make an offering in thanks. He chucked her chin with one scarred knuckle. "I think I can clean it after it dries, and it will be no worse for the wear and will make for a nice tale. Rescued by Opes, the sweet Nereid who rescued me from the sea's clutches."

"Opis, Hebrides."

"Eh?"

"My name, it's Opis. Not Opes." Or Opas.

"Ah, yes, sorry. Slip of the tongue." He lifted a pouch and poured the contents into his hand. "See these ivory dice? They're very worn around the edges. This man loved his games very much. But Tyche didn't love him back as much, seeing how little wealth he held."

She smiled at the little joke with the goddess of fortune, the eldest daughter of the Titan, Oceanus.

Hebrides glanced at the sun. "Time to go. Keep looking, Opes. I'm sure you'll find it. In the meantime, you've given me much happiness with what you have found."

She didn't correct him again. He was likely just distracted by his hopes that Tyche would show him fortune. "And have the men claimed what I found? Or did you offer it to the temple?"

"Oh, it's been claimed. Every bit." He chucked her chin again and smiled down at her, his teeth gleaming through the curls of his beard.

She'd seen herself reflected in his eyes and smiled back, her heart racing like dolphins pulled along in the wake of a ship.

The moon was two days from full and painted the sea in broken reflections of herself on the dancing waves.

Opis had finished her sacred duties and spent the rest of the day searching the sea bottom for Hebrides's pouch. She'd found it along with several interesting rings and a handful of tiny glass bottles, the lids still waxed securely shut.

She assumed her mortal aspect and climbed ashore, balancing as she moved from rock to rock until she reached the verge of the beach. She hadn't realized she'd searched for so long. There was no chance she'd see him this late. He was probably in the barracks at the village.

She had only ever been up to the village and Poseidon's temple once, and that was when they'd been building the first stone temple of plain rocks and rubble. Men were only learning how to work with stone buildings then. This new one with its tall columns gleamed, visible for several *stadia* as Apollo rode his golden chariot over the promontory.

During the day, the entire area buzzed with activity, priests shouting instructions to workers, scribes making notes of inventory and payment schedules, slaves working the stone and muscling it into place.

She'd always admired mortals for their skills and imagination. The gods took their sacrifices as a matter of course, having been worshipped for thousands of years, never thinking of the effort that went into them.

That reminded her. Hebrides would make a sacrifice to her tomorrow night! What would it be? A suckling pig? A kid? A dove, perhaps? Yes, a dove would be quite nice.

She rounded a rock and nodded to a tree nymph resting on a branch of her tree.

She heard a murmur. What was that? It sounded like Hebrides! What luck! She could see him without having to go to the village, which she'd been dreading, hating the busy-ness men and their cacophony of noises.

"Yes, I have the little chit scouring the bottom of the sea for treasures," Hebrides said as she approached. "She's looking for a pair of new dice. How many soldiers have dice in their pouches? She'll be bringing me riches for a long time. I had to get a new pouch to hold everything."

What? Opis stopped, standing behind a laurel tree, her joy dying in her breast. She peered out into the night, searching for him.

"How long do you think before she catches on?" another voice, heavily accented, asked. "You didn't have a thing to your name but your sword and *aspis*."

"Probably as long as I want, the way love shimmers in the girl's eyes."

Laughter from the accented man. "Women have always fallen from the sky for you, and now they rise from the sea, too. Tyche loves you,

Hebrides. Don't forget, though. The immortals are fickle, and they care little for us except what we sacrifice and how we entertain them."

Opis's heart fell, the blood drained from her face. She put her hand to her mouth to stifle the mixed cry of outrage and heartbreak that climbed up her throat.

"I have silly Opu well in hand. She makes those moon eyes, and I know she'd like me to dally with her. But she smells of fish and salt. No, I have only to make her a sacrifice tomorrow night in thanks for saving me, and I can work on cementing her patronage without having to make time with her. I already got a lamb the priests rejected from their last sacrifice. It's got a broken leg, but once I slit its throat and skin it, the bones wrapped in the hide on the fire will burn, whole or not."

Opis sucked in a breath beneath her hand. He would deliberately offer a soiled sacrifice intended to give thanks for his own rescue?

The other man laughed again. "You dance too close to edge of the gods' notice for me. Just don't give her a child. She'll chase after you the way Anonis did."

Hebrides made a growling sound. "I put paid to that easily enough. No reason to chase me when there's no brat to whine about, eh?"

"May Artemis never hear you speak, my friend. We better get up to the *stoa* and collect our wages and find out what shift that pizzle Ditinos gave us."

The men left, and Opis shrank back behind the tree, her fist pressed to her mouth. The fury and disgust at his betrayal mixed with shame at her naivete.

She and her sisters saved mortals. They did favors for them; they led them to the best fishing. They asked little in return, finding pleasure in the deed itself.

Opis had never thought about what the mortals might think of her sisters' succor. She had never considered that they might use that kindness to enrich themselves.

She clenched the bag in her hands. He'd been using her. Using her to enrich himself, not helping others regain their lost riches. He'd probably given nothing back to the temple.

Well, he'd pay for this. She turned and practically flew back to the water. Once in, she let the pouch drop back to the sea where it belonged, and changed back, flipping her tail hard as she dove.

She knew just who to talk to.

Oceanus's palace was in a grotto adorned with shells and pearls. Bright fish swam in and out of the courtyards and windows.

She scarcely answered her cousin titans when they greeted her, brushing them off distractedly as she made her way through the winding halls to Tyche's apartments. She scratched at the door.

"Enter, Opis," the goddess of fortune said.

Tyche reclined on a couch of carved coral. Her crown lay on a round table with swooping legs, reminiscent of unfurling octopus arms.

Opis made a quick bow in recognition of the goddess's primacy.

"What brings you to my father's palace?"

At her words, the dam broke. All of Opis's fury and shame boiled out. "I saved him," she growled. "He would have died. And he's not grateful. He's using me to enrich himself. Because I'm ignorant of mortals' wicked ways."

"Oh, dear Opis. Your ignorance is solely because you're young and innocent. Sit down, my sweet."

Opis sat on a chair made of giant fish bones and covered in seaweed cushions.

"Have you ever interacted with those you rescued before?"

"No." She had always just gotten them to the beach or another ship.

"So, you have learned a very important lesson in this, little Opis. Mortals can be cunning, even more so than the gods. Unlike the gods, they will not always be bound by their oaths. And the words that fall from their mouths will often play games, hiding their meaning in the shadows of what is not said, or in the way they are twisted."

"I am so ashamed," Opis said. "I thought he liked me. I thought I was helping him." She met Tyche's gaze. "I want to punish him."

"Ah, so you'll step fully into your role as an immortal. How do you want to punish him?"

"He spoke of fortune and how some are not loved by you, no matter how much they love you. His friend spoke of his fortune with women. He thought he was fortunate in manipulating me to acquire Poseidon's rightful offerings. I want him to see that favor turn to disfavor. In everything he does. I want him to rue the day I rescued him."

Tyche grinned. "You have a poetic side, Opis. I shall grant your desire. He'll be punished so completely that even his passage coin across the River Styx shall fall from his grasp and disappear into those dark depths and he'll be forced to linger there forever, always knowing he brought this on himself. Because you'll tell him, won't you, sweetling?"

Opis thought her mouth might break her smile was so hard as she reveled in the pleasure revenge and punishment brought her.

"I will, and I thank you. If there's ever a favor I can do in return, I'll do it."

Tyche smiled, her teeth gleaming. "Go with my blessings, then, dear Opis. Enjoy your judgment."

The nearly full moon made the sea look covered in silver, forever breaking into argent shards and reforming. Opis stood up straight as she walked toward the fire that Hebrides had built. The altar was crude, made of a flattish stone laid upon two blocky boulders. Nothing lay smoking upon it; the smell of fresh blood was conspicuously absent.

Opis covered her mouth with a hand lest he see her smirk as he saw her.

"Oh, Opas, you're here. I, I'm not ready. I've had some difficulties." He smiled ruefully as he gestured at the empty altar.

"I see. What happened?"

"Well, my lamb ran off and as I chased it, I tripped on a root, and a dog caught the damned thing. I tried to get the dog to let go, but he bit me." He lifted a hand wrapped in a rag.

"Hmmm," Opis said blandly. "I wouldn't think he'd be able to run very well with a broken leg."

"What? How... No. He was fine," he blustered.

"Then you lied to your friend about cementing your patronage to silly Opu?"

He blinked and gabbled excuses. More lies. Opis let him run down.

"You sought to deceive me, Hebrides. You used my willingness to help you regain your possessions as a way to enrich yourself."

"I never, dear Opes. You saved me. I'd be at the bottom of the ocean if you hadn't brought me to the shore and cradled me against your breast."

Opis shook her head in disgust. "Yes, you're so grateful you cannot remember my name. But I promise you, you'll wish you had gone to the bottom of the sea. And you will remember my name from here out."

"What? Why are you being like this? This is all a misunderstanding."

"Yes. You misunderstood who I am. I am not some weak and silly mortal girl. I am Opis, a Titan, descended from the first gods." She let the mortal aspect fall away, allowing her immortal aspect to illuminate her as she rose to half her actual height. She kept her legs so she would remain regal. The moon shone down on her and she glowed with her power.

She glared down at him, smiling as his eyes went pleasingly large. His mouth dropped open, and she savored his realization that he had made a mistake. A very large and irredeemable mistake.

"Great lady," he said, dropping to his knees. "I beg your forgiveness."

She smiled a smile sharp enough to cut. "I will not give it. No, I will punish you. You insulted me, took advantage of my kindness, and failed to give Poseidon his due, keeping it to enrich yourself. I spoke to my cousin Tyche, the goddess of fortune that you men seem to love to chase. She has cursed you, Hebrides. Everything you do now will fail you. That lamb that escaped you? Just the beginning. Tyche's disfavor will follow you for the rest of your life. And when you arrive at Hades's threshold, do not think you'll finally be safe from my vengeance or her curse."

Hebrides's face had fallen as she spoke. Real fear and rue washed over his face as he heard her words. But he had no idea what it meant. Not yet.

She wished she could watch, but she heard her father's conch horn calling his daughters. Some tragedy at sea to attend to.

"I would say farewell, but I know you will not fare well at all. You may think to sacrifice to Tyche for forgiveness, but it will be for naught. And lest you think to appeal to another god, remember: no god can intervene in another's curse. You have no succor, Hebrides. Think on that when you remember the day you played on the heart of a Titan who meant only to rescue and help you in your second chance at life."

She strode away through the trees, growing so that the tops brushed her palms as she walked.

Once at the shore, she entered the sea and transformed into her water aspect, heading to where her sisters worked rescuing sailors from the sea.

The ship had struck a rock and was sinking. The crew and passengers were jumping into the water, some carrying bags they hoped to save with themselves.

She approached her third man as he flailed in the water, trying to stay afloat. Opis changed into her mortal aspect and took the man by the hair. "Don't struggle. I'm here to help you."

He relaxed when he realized she really was pulling him toward the shore.

A scent of cinnamon and rank sweat filled the air. She pulled the sailor closer to him and sniffed. Yes, it was coming from him.

None of the others she had rescued smelled like this.

But Hebrides had the same scent. Was this the scent of a duplicitous mortal?

She had pushed the man beneath the surface before she realized she'd done it. He struggled, but he was no match for her. She let him go when he went limp. He rose slowly and bobbed on the water.

There. The world would be safe from a wicked, deceitful mortal. Perhaps some little babe in arms would live to grow up without suffering at the hands of such a one.

A few fish were already circling. They would feast well tonight.

She turned and headed for another mortal splashing in the sea.

What would they smell like?

About the Author

Lois Tilton of Locus called Thea Hutcheson's work in Realms of Fantasy's 100th issue "sensual, fertile, with seed quickening on every page. Well done..." Her work has appeared in places such as *Hot Blood XI*, *Fatal Attractions*; *The Best of Baen's Universe*; *High Noon on Proxima B*; and several of the critically acclaimed Fiction River anthologies.

She lives in a house with four rescue cats, a goat herding dog, and an understanding housemate in an economically depressed, unscenic, nearly historic small city in Colorado. When she's not writing, she serves as a factotum.

Find more of her work at www.theahutcheson.com

About the Editor

*J*essica Guernsey writes Fantasy and Sci-Fi short stories. With a BA in Journalism from Brigham Young University and a MA in Publishing from Western Colorado University, her work is published in magazines and anthologies. By day, she crushes dreams as a slush pile reader for multiple publishers. By night, she edits and produces anthologies. Frequently, she can be found at writing conferences. She isn't difficult to spot; just look for the extrovert.

While she spent her teenage angst in Texas, she now lives on a mountain in Utah with her family and a bossy mini schnauzer.

Discover more stories at jessicaguernsey.com.

Additional Copyright Information